KYLE'S
JOURNEY

BY M. LEE PRESCOTT

Published by Mt. Hope Press

Copyright 2018, M. Lee Prescott

ISBN: 978-0-9982184-5-8

AUTHOR WEBSITE: http://www.mleeprescott.com/

This book is a work of fiction. Names, characters, places, and events are products of the author's imagination or are used fictitiously. Any resemblance to actual people (alive or deceased), locales, or events is entirely coincidental.

For Abby, Ava, Benjamin and Teddy, and their incredible parents

CHAPTER 1

Harriet Winthrop walked arm in arm with her mother, Helen, as they deplaned at the Grenville Airport. After a year of listening to her mother's stories about Saguaro Valley, she was curious, but also wary. Shy and introverted, she did not go comfortably into new situations. Meeting new people was always a challenge unless they were ten years old or younger.

"There's Spark," her mother said, waving to a tall man in a Stetson who bore an uncanny resemblance to the actor and politician Fred Thompson. Spark Foster stood next to an enormous SUV parked at the side of the tarmac, a driver by his side.

"Don't they know we have to go through baggage?" Harriet whispered.

"They'll handle it, you'll see," Helen said, patting her arm as they neared the two men. "Just give Jimmy the claim checks."

Mouth agape, Harriet watched her normally reserved mother throw her arms around Fred Thompson, who scooped her up and gave her a twirl. "Hello, hello, welcome back!"

After setting Helen down, he turned to Harriet. Before her mother could introduce them, he grabbed Harriet in a bear hug. "Just as beautiful as your ma. Welcome to the Valley!"

"Thank you, Mr. Foster. So nice to meet you at last."

He released her. "Pleasure's all mine, darlin', but there are no Mr. Fosters here. Please call me Spark. And this is Jimmy. He'll collect your bags if you give him the claim checks."

Jimmy disappeared around the side of their plane, and the trio stood chatting as planes flew in and departed. Grenville was a country airport with several runaways, acres of hangars, and a stable of private jets and small planes. The terminal building reminded Harriet of a drive-in hamburger place back home. She had researched Spark Foster on the internet and knew he was a billionaire with a host of alternative energy companies all over the world. As they stood in a spot that would clearly be off-limits in any other airfield, she wondered if the Grenville Airport was one of his holdings.

"It's so nice of you to have me," she said.

"Our pleasure. Can't wait to show you around."

Helen smiled up at him. "Are you sure we won't be interlopers at the wedding? I mean... I barely know Polly or Kevin."

"Not a bit of it. They're both thrilled to have you here, as are all our friends. Ben and Leonora are about to bust a gasket, they're so excited. We're invited to dinner there tonight."

"How lovely," Helen said as Jimmy appeared with their bags.

"Prepare yourself, darlin'," Spark said, winking at Harriet. "There's nothin' like a Morgan family dinner. I think they'll all be there except Sam and Rose, who'll be flyin' in tomorrow in time for the rehearsal dinner."

Helen laughed. "He's right about that, sweetheart. Morgan dinners are like nothing you've ever experienced."

*****

As they drove up the drive to the Morgan's Run Big House, home to Spark's dear friends Ben and Leonora Morgan, Harriet gazed up in wonder. "Oh my, this is a beautiful spot." She had barely gotten over her awe of Spark's rambling estate and now, driving through the gates of Morgan's Run, she was thunderstruck at the beauty of the vast ranch property. The Big House was on a smaller scale than Spark's colossus, but the setting was lovely and the views spectacular. "I was expecting desert."

"It's our orographic effect," Spark said, referring to the unusual cloud formation and abundant moisture that had created this extraordinary green valley. For the most part, tourists had not discovered the Valley, which suited its three-thousand year-round residents. The Morgans, their neighbors to the south, Martha and Jay Dillon, and a few other ranchers owned most of the valley land. Ben Morgan Senior had sold a thirty-acre parcel to Spark, his college roommate and lifelong friend, but then he was family. Valley land rarely changed hands outside the families.

"I've never heard of that," Harriet said, gazing around at their verdant surroundings.

"Most people haven't," Spark said. "It's made it possible for my buddy, and now his daughters Ruthie and Beth, to operate the largest, most successful organic farm in the southwest. Can't wait to show you Valley Stables too. We've got green grass that gives Kentucky bluegrass a run for its money."

Spark parked his Mercedes SUV and led them around the side of the house. It was a beautiful evening, warm with clear skies. No sooner had they rounded the house than a tall, slender sixty-something with sky-blue eyes and a full head of salt-and-pepper hair waved and called, "Hey, there you are! Welcome, welcome!"

Ben Morgan Senior stepped off the terrace to greet them, a petite beautiful blonde in white capris and cotton sweater of swirling blues and greens at his side. Behind them followed the only other person on the terrace, a drop-dead-handsome, dark-haired man. Ben Senior, then his wife, Leonora, hugged Helen, then turned to Harriet with effusive welcomes.

Their companion hung back. His smile was enough to take Harriet's breath away. She was still breathless when Leonora Morgan said, "And, Harriet this is our youngest boy, Kyle."

"Hey, great to see you, Helen," he said, hugging her mother, then turning to her. "And great to meet you, Harriet." He held out his hand, which Harriet took.

His firm handshake sent ripples of electricity from her head to her toes. She managed to mumble, "Hello," as they released each other's hand.

"Are you all right, darlin'?" Leonora said. "Your face is red as a beet."

Harriet shook her head. "Thank you, I'm fine. Must be the heat."

As they were swept up onto the terrace, her mother gave her a quizzical look. When Harriet passed Kyle Morgan, she noticed he was grinning. *Oh Lord, what he must think of me!* No man had ever had that kind of effect on her, and she suspected he knew it. It didn't matter, though. Harriet had decided many years ago that no man would get close enough to hurt her the way she and her mother had been hurt. No one! Judson Winthrop, her father had been charming, handsome and kind at first, and look how he turned out! Then there was Louis. His treachery and betrayal still cut like a knife. *How could I have been so naïve and stupid?*

As they crossed the terrace to the bar, they were greeted by a taller, larger version of Kyle Morgan, the oldest Morgan sibling, Ben, and his wife, Maggie. Their children Emma and Ben the third were rolling around on the grass with the ranch dogs. "And that would be my youngest sister, Ruthie, wife and mother, still like one of the kids," Ben said, pointing to a beautiful redhead in jeans and ranch T-shirt, her hair in a lopsided ponytail. She ducked just as her nephew jumped over her, squealing with laughter, an Australian shepherd on his heels. A tall, lanky cowboy stood at the edge of the melee, cradling a baby on his hip. "That's my best buddy and now-brother-in-law, Harley Langdon," Ben continued. "And baby Charlotte, my newest niece."

Harriet smiled. Ben Morgan didn't have to add that Charlotte and Harley belonged to Ruthie. The baby's red curls and his adoring gaze told all.

"It's all a bit overwhelming at first," Maggie said. "But you get used to it."

"As if there's another choice," said a voice at their side. "Robbie Morgan," he said, extending his hand. "You must be Helen's daughter?"

She shook his hand. Unlike his brothers, Robbie was fair-haired like his mother. *Still drop-dead gorgeous, of course.*

"Yes. I'm Harriet. Hello. I've heard so much about you all."

"This is my better half, my fiancée Hope Seymour," Robbie added as a willowy woman with sandy hair in a braid down her back and deep blue eyes stepped forward.

As they shook hands, Harriet said, "Hello, Ms. Seymour, I am a great admirer of your work. I loved the painting Mother brought home last year."

"Thank you. Great to meet you, Harriet. How long are you staying?"

"Our tickets are open-ended, but I'd guess a couple of weeks. School's out for me, so I'm letting my mother set the agenda. She was very eager to come back and visit your parents and Spark."

"We're wondering if there might be something cookin' there," Ben said.

Harriet laughed. "Mother insists they're just friends. She's had a pretty rough few years, so this friendship has really perked her up."

Maggie patted her arm. "We'll keep her perked up, don't you worry. What can Ben get you to drink?"

The women asked for white wine, and the brothers headed to the bar. "Mother wasn't kidding when she said the Valley grows handsome men. Oh my goodness, look at them all," Harriet said, surprising herself at her saucy statement.

Maggie laughed. "Yes, they're quite a bunch."

"And here comes another one," Hope said. "The couple of the hour, Kevin Larrabee and Polly Granger."

"They look very happy," Harriet said, gazing at the broad-shouldered, sandy-haired man and the slender blonde beside him. He held a wriggling toddler who soon broke free and ran for the group on the lawn.

"Yes, and little Jasper is our Ben's best buddy. It's been great having him here."

"So they already have a child?" Harriet asked, smiling as the little boys greeted each other tumbling over in the grass.

"Jasper is Kevin's son," Maggie said. "He moved to the valley last winter after his mom died. Kind of a shock at first because Kevin never knew he had a son, but they've certainly become a family now, haven't they, Hope?"

Her companion nodded, smiling, but Harriet noticed that her eyes were sad. Her mother had told her a bit about Hope and Robbie's courtship and Hope's inability to bear children after a botched abortion. There was a fragility about Hope Seymour that Harriet understood. She had never lost a child or had such an experience as Hope, but she wanted to take her hand, to offer comfort.

"Quite a crew, isn't it?" a voice said beside them. Kyle Morgan addressed all three women, but his attention was clearly on Harriet, who found herself blushing.

"And, we're missing Lang and Beth and Rose and Sam," Maggie said, referring to Beth and Sam Morgan and their respective spouses. Beth and Lang lived just south of the ranch, and Sam and Rose in Maryland.

"I know Sam and Rose get in tomorrow," Hope said, "but where are Lang, Beth, and Lily tonight?"

"The Dillons. Jaybo wasn't well enough to come, and Martha asked if they'd help out." The Morgans' close friends Martha and Jaybo Dillon owned Saguaro Valley Winery. He was always ailing with one complaint or the other after a lifetime of alcoholism. Lang had escaped the Valley to Boston, but when he returned for a visit, he fell in love with the eldest Morgan daughter and that was that. Rose, his younger sister, who had spent many years caring for her parents, was now free to take her dream job in Baltimore. Sam Morgan, her husband, had joined a prestigious Baltimore architectural firm.

"Here you go, ladies," Ben Morgan said as he and Robbie distributed drinks. They each had a beer, as did Kyle, who was now standing almost shoulder to shoulder with Harriet. His nearness was both disquieting and comforting. *What is happening? No, no, no!*

From across the terrace, Leonora Morgan clapped her hands. "Okay, okay, everybody! Grab your drinks, find a seat, get your plate, and dig in! Carmela has outdone herself again!"

Harriet started toward her mother's group but was immediately waylaid by Ben Morgan. "Come sit with us," he said. "With any luck, Ruthie'll take our kids to sit with the grandparents, and we'll have some peace and quiet."

Maggie elbowed her husband as they strolled to the second of two long tables festooned with Leonora's colorful linens and set with her brightly patterned collection of Southwestern pottery.

Harriet felt like she'd stepped into a spread for *House Beautiful*.

Your mom's fine," Kyle said, gently touching her elbow, sending shivers through her. "Come sit with us."

Oh boy! Harriet thought as she allowed herself to be led into a fairy tale.

Chapter 2

Buffet tables groaned with food—platters of trout, strip steaks, chicken, and grilled portabellas. An array of salads was placed between the entrees—Southwestern chopped salad with creamy cilantro dressing, taco salad with Carmela's special dressing, huge bowls of green salads tossed with colorful nasturtium flowers, and grilled potato salad. Baskets of Carmela's breads, butters, and flavored oils were set out on the tables.

As Harriet stared, uncertain of where to begin, Kyle said, "Don't be scared. Just jump right in. That's what we do." She gave him a wan smile as she picked up a serving fork and selected a piece of trout garnished with tomatoes and cilantro.

He watched her, marveling at her slender, delicate hands and arms, her look of astonishment at each dish she noticed. While not a conventional beauty, Harriet Winthrop was arresting. There was a singularity about her carriage and the intensity of her every movement. He'd dated a lot of women over the years, but none as interesting as this one. According to his mother, Harriet was thirty-five, six years older than he was. That made her all the more interesting. *No ties, no strings, no attachments* had been his motto for so long that it had become a way of life. Somehow, he knew that any involvement with Harriet Winthrop would have mega strings, even if she lived three thousand miles away. *Whoa, boy*, he thought as he followed her along the buffet, then back to their table.

The conversation at the table was lively as Ben related hilarious stories about a recent pack trip. It had been a group of executives, most of whom were inexperienced riders, so their guides—Ben, Harley and Robbie—were kept on their toes. At one point, after an amusing description of Harley and one of the women riders, Kevin asked, "Why didn't Barnes go on the trip? I thought he'd kind of taken over now that Harley's up at the thoroughbred farm."

"School," Maggie said. "He had exams, so Harley, our savior, offered to fill in." Jeb Barnes, Maggie's assistant at the ranch stables, was married to Spark's daughter Amy. At her encouragement, Jeb had returned to school to complete an engineering degree.

"How are things at the swishy new farm anyway?" Robbie asked, turning to Kyle.

"Pretty good. First horses arrive next week. We're keyed."

"You're the veterinarian, I understand," Harriet said, turning to him.

As their eyes met, Kyle swallowed, lost for a second in hers. *What is it about this woman?* He stammered, "Yup, that's me," thinking that he must sound like a complete idiot. Proximity to Harriet Winthrop made his pulse race and sent his libido into overdrive. He hadn't dated, really, since Boston. He and Dara Littlefield, Maggie's friend, had had a few dinners and gone to the movies, but they were never going to be anything but pals. Aria Firorelli, Spark's chef, had cajoled him into taking her dancing one night, but that ended with her heading out of the local saloon on the arm of a cowboy, leaving Kyle and some of his coworkers playing pool and drinking too much. Lost in thought, he suddenly realized she'd asked him a question, and he hadn't a clue what she'd said.

"Are you okay?" Harriet asked,

"Sorry, I'm a space cadet tonight. What was your question?"

She smiled, a warm, wonderful smile. "No question. I just said that must be a big job at such a large facility. I'm looking forward to Spark's tour."

"Oh, when's that happening?"

"I believe the plan is for us to come out tomorrow morning."

"I'll look for you. Happy to show you around the barn and treatment rooms."

She lowered her eyes. "Thanks."

Hope gazed over at the couple and said, "So, Harriet, what do you do back home?"

"I'm a teacher. Fifth grade at a small Quaker school just outside of Horseshoe Crab Cove where my mother lives."

"Do you live with your mom?" Maggie asked.

"No, Hampton Meeting is a boarding school, ages seven to eighteen. I was a dorm parent in one of the houses for the youngest students, but now I live in a house on campus. I still fill in at the dorm when needed."

"Wow, that's young, isn't it?" Robbie said.

"Yes, we're one of the last schools to take elementary-aged children. We have a long waiting list."

"I can't imagine sending Emma away," Maggie said.

Her husband nodded. "No way, Jose."

Harriet nodded. "It's a wonderful school, and we do everything we can to make it homey and warm, but I wouldn't recommend it. Many of the students' parents are diplomats or celebrities and business people who travel constantly. For them, it's either full-time nannies or boarding school."

"Our parents would've busted a gourd before they'd have let any of us out of their sight before college," Kyle said, just as Emma and her brother hid behind his chair. He pretended not to notice for about twenty seconds, then turned to Harriet with a grin. "Excuse me, I've got some monsters to capture." With a roar, he jumped up and chased after them.

"Never grew up," Ben said. "He and Ruthie are the Peter Pan and Wendy of the family."

Maggie patted his shoulder. "Except that Wendy did grow up."

"Sort of," her husband said, pointing as Ruthie hopped up from her seat and joined Kyle in the chase.

Leonora appeared at the head of the table, shaking her head. "Can't one of you do something about your crazy brother and sister? Look at them!" She waved her hand, and they gazed over to spy Ruthie and Kyle rolling around on the grass with their niece and nephew. "Crazy, those two. Anyway, I'm here to say that desserts are out. Don't hurry with dinner. Have seconds and thirds, but wanted you to know that Carmela just set out dessert and coffee at the table near the door." She walked around and smiled down at Harriet. "How you doin', sweetie? I hope my hellions aren't driving you crazy."

"I'm fine, thank you. What a delicious meal."

"Carmela is a genius. Don't tell Spark," she whispered, "but I think she runs circles around his fancy Portland chef."

"I don't know, Ma," Robbie said, winking at Harriet. "Aria's made some pretty spectacular meals."

His mother waved her hand. "Oh, pish, tush! Now let me grab a hold of your silly sister before she hurts herself, and then who'll take care of baby Charlotte?"

Ben grinned. "Shortcake can hold her own. It's your idiot fifth child I'd be more concerned about. He's more delicate than the rest of us."

Leonora threw up her hands. "Oh, Harriet, what you must think of us! See what I have to put up with?" She hurried off toward the lawn.

"She loves every minute of it," Maggie said as they watched Leonora waving her arms to no avail.

Later, sated and sleepy, Harriet and Helen said their goodbyes, hugging the elder Morgans and saying good night to the others. "I'm so sorry you're not staying with us this visit," Leonora said, "but Spark thought you'd be more comfortable over there. Goodness knows he has plenty of bedrooms. But we do too, if you want a change of scenery. Sam and Rose can always stay with her parents or with Lang and Beth."

"Thanks, Mrs. Morgan."

"Leonora, please. No surnames here."

Spark approached and said his goodbyes. Kyle stood nearby, studying Harriet, wondering what to say. Finally, he said, "Hey, Spark, you must be out straight tomorrow. Why don't I give the ladies the grand tour?"

Surprised, his mother turned. "That's very nice of you, honey."

"You sure?" Spark said.

Kyle grinned. "Glad to."

"Well, I do have a few items on my agenda."

Kyle turned to Helen and Harriet. "Then it's settled. What time would you like me to pick you up?"

"Don't you have to be at work early?" Harriet asked.

"Tomorrow's flexible."

Helen watched the interplay between her second child and Kyle Morgan before saying, "That would be lovely, Kyle. Thank you. Would ten suit you?"

"Perfect. I'll be at Casa Grande at ten."

"Well, then, good night," Harriet said, smiling at him and their hosts.

Later, as Harriet hugged her mother good night, Helen said, "Kyle Morgan's nice, isn't he?"

Harriet blushed. "They're *all* nice."

"Hmm, maybe some more than others," Helen said. "Good night, sweetheart."

CHAPTER 3

True to his word, Kyle greeted them in Spark's huge kitchen on the dot of ten. "Ready, ladies?"

Aria, who had been preparing food at one end, sidled up to stand beside him. "If you wait ten minutes, Spark asked me to pack some sandwiches and things. It's such a beautiful day, you might want to picnic." Harriet and her mother were both in the room, but Aria's gaze and her remarks were directed at Kyle.

"Got it covered," Kyle said, grinning at Harriet. "Carmela was up at dawn and has sent enough to feed an army."

Aria shrugged and returned to her work without a word.

"I think we're all set, right, Mom?" Harriet said.

Helen stood next to her, purse in hand, light sweater over her arm. "You know, honey, I'm feeling a little tired this morning. I think I'll stay here, rest, and enjoy a book on Spark's beautiful sunporch."

Harriet gazed at her in surprise. Ten minutes ago, her mother had been frisky as a new colt. *What is she up to?* "Shall I stay with you? We can do this another time."

"Absolutely not! You've got all that food to eat and a handsome man to squire you around. Go, have fun. *You* can give *me* the tour in a few days."

Harriet was about to protest when Spark walked in. "You young'uns go on and have fun. I'll check in on your ma."

"I thought you had a million errands in town," Aria called from the far end of the island, where she was chopping vegetables.

Spark winked at them. "Always have time for a pretty lady. Now scoot, you two. I'm right behind you. I won't be long, and Aria's here."

"Oh, my heavens, you make me sound like an invalid. Shoo, the bunch of you!" Helen said, waving her hands.

"Not sure what that was about," Kyle said as they headed down the front walk.

"I do, but it's not worth discussing," she replied. "Oh, what a beautiful morning!"

"Most mornings in the Valley are. Might get a downpour later in the day, but the mornings are usually just like this."

"You're lucky. It was thick fog and rainy when I left home. Thanks," she added as he opened the truck door for her. Unlike most of Spark's oversized vehicles, this was a small Tacoma with an extended cab. She gazed behind her and saw a very large picnic basket. "Your Carmela really was expecting an army, wasn't she?"

He laughed. "Believe me, after we're done, I'll spread this out in the dining hall and it'll be gone in less than five minutes. Our cook isn't due to arrive until next week, so the guys have been fending for themselves. It's not a pretty sight."

"Are you sure you have time for this?" she asked as they headed down the drive.

"Happy to do it. It's an amazing place. Just you wait."

*****

After Kyle drove her by the south end of Morgan's Run to show her Ben and Maggie's house, they drove out of the ranch and turned south, driving the short distance to Saguaro Valley Winery. Kyle pointed out the Dillons' house, then turned up a driveway that led to Lang and Beth's home. "Oh my goodness," she said. "I feel like I'm at home."

"That was Lang's intention. He loves Cape Cod and the islands."

"Your family has certainly built some beautiful homes. The location of Maggie and Ben's is spectacular," she said.

"And you haven't even seen their view to the west. We'll get you up there soon. That was the original farmhouse, built by my grandparents. Ben and my brother Sam designed the renovation as a surprise for Maggie. It's three times as large as it was."

"She must have been amazed."

"That's how he proposed."

"How romantic. What if she'd said no?"

"He would have dogged her every step till she changed her mind. He was and is crazy about her."

After exiting the winery, he headed north for the fifteen-minute drive to Valley Stables. They toured the stables, barns, and his office and treatment areas, Kyle providing running commentary throughout. Finally, they made a quick tour of the bunkhouses and dining hall. "What do you think?" he asked, turning to her. "You hungry?"

"Actually, yes," she said.

"We could eat inside or just take a few things and go sit on the hilltop in the shade."

"I vote for hilltop in the shade, but can I use your facilities first?"

"Restroom's just inside the door, but I can't vouch for its cleanliness. Our cleaning crew starts next week too."

"I'll be fine."

"I'm gonna grab the basket from the truck. Be right back," he said, turning to go. "Unless you want me to wait so no one barges in on you?"

Harriet smiled that beautiful smile that made him want to pull her into his arms. "No, of course not! I can take care of myself."

"Okay, but don't say I didn't warn you."

After laying out the food on one of the dining hall tables, they took their choices outside in the sunshine. Kyle grabbed a blanket from the truck, and they walked up the rise to a shady spot from which one could see for miles in three directions down and across the wide grassy valley to mountains in the north, east, and south. "Oh my," Harriet sighed as she settled on the blanket. We don't have views like this at home."

"Yeah, but you have the ocean."

"There is that."

"And the Berkshires."

"Yes, I love it out there. I went to school in western Massachusetts and got my first teaching job in Holyoke."

"Where'd you go? To school, I mean."

"First to a boarding school in Northampton. That school's closed now. Then to Smith."

"So you were a boarder too?"

She nodded. "Not at such a young age as my students, although I should have gone sooner."

"Oh?"

"Home life was a horror show. Not my mom. She's always been a rock, but our father was an abusive alcoholic."

"That must've been rough."

"You are so lucky. Your parents are great. And Spark too."

"Yeah, we're pretty fortunate," he said.

"Not everyone's that lucky."

"I'm sorry, Harriet."

"Long time ago. Now, enough about me. Tell me about your life, medical school, the farm, anything."

He wanted to ask more but knew better, especially after glimpsing the pain in her eyes.

He spent the next hour regaling her with stories of life growing up on the ranch, his time in veterinary school, and his hopes for the future. "I came back because I missed home and the Valley, but there was a lot I loved about the East

Coast. This job," he said, waving his arm toward the farm complex, "was too hard to pass up. I figure I'll help them set up, see how this life suits me, then decide. My dad calls me the nomadic Morgan. My itinerant lifestyle pisses him off 'cause he likes us all settled and close by, preferably under one roof."

"That might be difficult with your growing family."

He grinned. "Yeah, the next generation's booming, and you haven't even met little Lily yet, have you?"

"Your sister Beth's daughter?"

He nodded. "She's a pistol."

"I'd love to pop over and see them all at the ranch day care. Polly and Lynn invited me to come."

"Quite a scene, I understand. My nephew Bennie and his buddy Jasper, Kevin's son, are the ringleaders of a rough gang."

"Cute, I'm sure."

"Yeah, I love 'em all," he said, his voice softening. "Especially Em. She's an amazing little girl with the courage and heart of a lion."

"Mother told me a little about her surgeries and recovery."

"That baby worked so hard to make her parents happy. We were all rooting for her, that's for sure. Maggie Williams was the best thing that ever happened to my brother. Talk about lucky."

"Yes, they seem very happy together."

"How about you? Is there a guy in your life?"

"No."

"I'm surprised."

"It's been a conscious choice for a lot of reasons." Abruptly, Harriet stood and gathered her sandwich wrappers, napkin, and empty ice tea bottle. "You know what? I think I should be getting back, and I'm sure you have lots of work to do."

"No rush. I'm pacing myself for the onslaught next week."

"Still, I should get back to Mother."

He stood and gently reached to touch her arm. "I'm sorry. My family calls me and my brother Ben nosey parkers for a reason. I didn't mean to pry."

Helen stiffened, pulling out of his grasp. "It's okay, really. I just want to get back." Without another word, she turned and started walking toward the truck.

Kyle gathered the blanket and the rest of their things and followed, wondering what the hell he'd stumbled into. When she reached the truck, she turned and waited for him.

"Lemme just grab Carmela's basket and I'll be right out," he said, throwing the blanket into the bed of the truck.

Harriet nodded. "I'll wait here."

When he returned, she was sitting in the truck, gazing straight ahead. "All set?" he asked as he slid into the driver's seat. Harriet nodded but didn't meet his eye.

He put the key in the ignition and was about to start the truck, when she said, "Wait, Kyle, I'm sorry. That was childish and extremely rude of me. A button got pushed, and I reacted badly."

"No problem. We all have buttons. I shouldn't have pried."

"You were just being friendly, and I acted like a lunatic. Please forgive me."

She gazed over at him with soft eyes, and he grinned. "Nothing to forgive. Now let's get you back to Casa Grande."

"Does Spark call it that?"

"Never, and don't tell him I do. He never does anything that's not supersized."

Kyle pointed out the sights on the drive back, finally pulling into Spark's drive a little after two.

Harriet hopped out and turned to say goodbye. "Thanks, this was really nice. After the wedding, I'll bring Mother out."

"Horses'll be there and so will I. See you at the rehearsal tomorrow if not before?"

"Yes, thanks again," she said, waving before turning to walk to the front door. *Do I need an emergency call to Elise?* she thought, wondering if her therapist would be available. She hadn't reacted like today since she was starving herself to death along with a host of other self-destructive behaviors. *I can't go back to that, or I'll kill myself this time.*

CHAPTER 4

After Harriet and Kyle's departure, Helen had taken a walk. When she returned, Aria told her Leonora had phoned. She dialed the Big House, and her friend picked up on the first ring. "Hello, dearie," Leonora said. "Would you like to go into town for lunch? Ben is helping Spark with who knows what, and I thought we could catch up."

An hour later, they sat in Gracie's, the popular diner run by its six-foot namesake. The woman herself appeared in a soiled apron, wiry hair flecked with flour, and took their orders. She recommended the fish tacos, which they both ordered. As Gracie disappeared, Helen said, "She's something, isn't she?"

"Woman's a perfect disgrace, but she's also a love, and her food is divine."

They chatted about life, catching up since Helen's previous visit. "It's wonderful to meet your precious Harriet. I'd love it if all your girls would come out," Leonora said.

Helen smiled. "Maybe someday. They're all so busy."

"Are Lucy's your only grandchildren?"

"So far. My Lucy is alone at present. She and Rob decided to separate several months ago. It's been hard on the kids."

"Oh, honey, I'm so sorry. Any chance of reconciliation?"

"I'm not hopeful. Rob had an affair. I believe he's still seeing the woman."

"Oh, how awful for Lucy."

"It was her decision. She felt that even if he agreed not to see this person, these days with the internet, texting, and all that the affair would never really end,. It's been very hard on the kids. It's a small town and he's still there. His business is there."

"And the woman?"

"She lives several towns over, but she's been around a good bit."

"Horrid for you and Lucy!" Leonora said, nodding as the waitress brought their iced teas.

Later, as they oohed and aahed over their tacos, Leonora asked, "How about Harriet? Does she have a significant other?"

Helen shook her head, her eyes sad. "I'm not sure she'll ever trust a man."

"Oh dear."

"She spent half her childhood hiding in the hall closet during Jud's drunken rages, then Louis. He was her boyfriend during college. Horrible man. He was fifteen years older than Harriet. She's always been attracted to much older men. Even in high school, she dated a local man eight years older. Anyway, Louis turned out to be a grifter. He worked with a woman he introduced as his sister. Between them, they took all Harriet's inheritance and left her in considerable debt. I offered to help her and her father too, but she was so ashamed. Just curled up inside herself and has never come out."

"Your poor baby."

"Yes, it was dreadful. Her solace has been teaching and her students. She has a wonderful therapist."

"Did they ever arrest Louis and his accomplice?"

"No. All the money was transferred out of the country. They just disappeared. We have the police and FBI still watching for them, but I doubt they'll ever find them."

"What was their scheme? If you don't mind my asking."

"Louis posed as head of an investment and securities group similar to that of his idol, Bernie Madoff."

"Oh dear!"

"Oh dear is right. Harriet was so infatuated that she just handed it all over. They were making plans to get married and build their dream house. Before her sisters and I heard anything about it, they had merged their bank accounts and put his name on Harriet's trust account. She inherited that when she turned twenty-two. The day after her birthday, he liquidated everything, wired it to the Cayman Islands, then disappeared. She came home and her apartment had been ransacked. Everything of value was gone, along with that despicable man."

"How terrible for her and for you."

"She went completely to pieces. Came home and spent six months in a darkened room. I could barely get her to eat. She lost thirty-five pounds before we coaxed her out."

"Poor thing. You know, Spark has contacts all over the world. I wouldn't be surprised if his people could root them out."

"I'm sure it's too late. It's been thirteen years."

"Still, you might have Harriet talk to him. He likes nothing better than to play the hero on a white horse, and he has the resources to do it." Leonora nodded at the waitress, handing her cash and the check. "All set, darlin'. Please tell Gracie everything was delicious." She turned back to Helen. "How about another iced tea?"

"That would be lovely, thanks."

"Talk to Spark."

"It's more complicated, I'm afraid. Bringing things into the open has never been helpful for Harriet. In addition to eating disorders, she self-mutilated as a child. In the darkness of her closet, she tore out chunks of her hair and cut herself with tiny scissors. No matter where we hid them, she'd find them."

"Oh, Helen, I'm so sorry."

"There was some of that when she came home after Louis too. I worry that it would be too big a risk to churn things up."

"Is that what her therapist would say?"

"I'm not sure, but as her mother, I can't take the chance."

Gracie appeared with another pitcher of iced tea. "How about more tea ladies?" she said as she poured.

"Thanks, Grace," Leonora said.

"Your tacos were delicious," Helen added.

The tall owner nodded. "Have a great afternoon, gals."

CHAPTER 5

Vermillion sparkled with strings of twinkle lights as the families and friends gathered for Kevin and Polly's rehearsal dinner. The farm-to-table restaurant nestled in the middle of a large farm south of the Valley was one of Kevin and Polly's favorite places. Since Spark insisted on hosting the wedding reception, tonight was a joint effort by the Larrabees and Grangers. They'd taken over the entire restaurant, and Francis Bissett, the Vermillion chef, had created a special menu for the evening. Edna, the owner, had overseen the decorations and the long barn looked magical.

Most of Kevin's and Polly's families were staying at the Lodge, Morgan's Run luxurious inn and spa. A few family and friends were also housed in ranch cabins, local B and Bs, and at Spark's. Ivy, Jasper's aunt, was staying with Kevin and Jasper, and other guests were scattered around at Beth and Lang's, Ruthie and Harley's, and even a couple at the Dillons' winery.

The Morgans arrived en masse, including Sam and Rose, who had come from Maryland. Harriet and Helen were already there when the family came in, and for a second, she mistook the dark-haired Sam Morgan for Kyle. His arm was around a slender ash blonde who smiled demurely at those around her. *I know how she feels,* Harriet thought as a tall, handsome man who could have been Kyle Morgan's twin leaned over to speak to her.

"That's Lang, Rose, Sam, and Beth," her mother said, noticing her gaze. Lang's wife, Beth, the oldest Morgan sister, had a toddler with golden curls on her hip. She handed the child to her husband and greeted Polly and Kevin, who stood just inside the door. Dark haired like her brothers, Beth Dillon was tall, lean, and lovely in a sleeveless sundress and sandals. Right behind her came Ben and Maggie and Emma, along with Kyle, a toddler squirming in his arms. The minute Bennie spotted his buddy Jasper standing with a pretty redhead, he jumped out of his uncle's arms and took off.

"I believe that's his aunt Ivy," Helen said. "The sister of Jasper's deceased mother."

"Does she live here?" Harriet asked as Ivy approached the Morgan group to say hello. She seemed most interested in Kyle, with whom she strolled off to the bar.

"It's quite a group, isn't it?" Phyllis Granger said, coming to stand beside mother and daughter. "I'm Polly's mom, and this is my husband, Perris. Our kids are scattered around here somewhere as well as the grandkids. They were very brave inviting children tonight."

Helen smiled, shaking their hands. "I believe this is how they do things in the Valley."

"Oh yes!" Phyllis said, turning to Harriet. "So glad to meet you fellow East Coasters! You're not far from us, I believe?"

"You're in Bristol, right?" Helen said.

Phyllis nodded.

"Horseshoe Crab Cove is only about thirty minutes from there."

"I've never heard of it. Have you, honey?" Phyllis asked, turning to her husband.

"Just this side of Brayton Point, right?" he said.

"Yes, that's right. Harriet lives in Hampton, the next town over."

"Oh boy, honey, looks like we're needed for hosting duties. We'll catch up with you ladies later, okay?"

Not waiting for a response, Phyllis dragged her husband toward the front of the room and the evening began. Helen and Harriet were seated with Spark and his family. Their table included Buck Foster, Spark's son from California, Buck's sister Amy and her husband, Jeb Barnes and their son, Toby, as well as Kevin Larrabee's two sisters, Gigi and Elaine, and his brother, Craig. Buck Foster sat on Harriet's right, and he proved a gentle, kind dinner companion who conversed easily between her and Gigi Larrabee on his other side.

The meal began with a cold leek soup, then grilled ranch quail, portabellas, and trout served with platters of roasted vegetables. A colorful garden salad of arugula and fennel with a fresh lemony dressing finished off the meal, after which the toasting began. Finally, waitstaff appeared with flaming baked Alaskas.

Kyle sat with his siblings but couldn't help stealing glances at Harriet throughout the meal. She intrigued him in a way no woman ever had. Each time he looked, she was talking with Buck Foster, which infuriated him. *Why?* As dinner ended, guests stood, chatting or strolling the Vermillion grounds in the growing twilight. Fireflies appeared like stars fallen from the skies, darting in the tall grasses at the edge of the lawn. Helen wandered off with Spark and was chatting with the elder Morgans. Harriet, Buck, and Gigi Larrabee walked along the yellow clay path that ringed the main houses, marveling at the beauty of the place.

"The northwest is gorgeous and green," Gigi said, "but somehow I didn't expect that here."

"Did someone explain the orographic business?" Buck asked. "It's kind of unusual."

"Yes, my brother filled us in. He seems as if he's here to stay, especially now with Polly. We've always hoped he'd come back to Portland eventually, especially now with Jasper. I'd love to be nearer my sweet, adorable nephew. Mom and Dad too."

"Things change and people move," a voice said from behind the trio as Kyle appeared.

"Did you meet Kyle Morgan?" Buck asked Gigi and Harriet, knowing full well Harriet, at least, had met him.

"No," Gigi gushed, extending her hand. "Another gorgeous Morgan! Only problem is you're all married."

Kyle gave Buck a sidelong glance before reaching to shake Gigi's hand. "Not this one. I'm the last of the single Morgan offspring."

Gigi's eyes sparkled. "Really?"

"Yeah, they all found the partners of their dreams. Robbie and Hope aren't married yet, but soon. Just look at them." He pointed ahead, where the couple walked arm in arm. Hope's head rested on her blond fiancé's shoulder as he rubbed her back.

Gigi batted her eyelashes. "Well, we'll just have to find *you* a woman of *your* dreams, won't we?"

Kyle laughed. "Don't waste your time there. I'm pretty hopeless in that department. However, if you're lookin' for eligible bachelors, there'll be plenty at the wedding. Valley Stables has a whole bunkhouse full of 'em. Men outnumber women in the Valley big-time."

"Oh my God—if they're half as cute as you, I'll be in heaven!" Before he knew what was happening, Gigi linked arms with Buck Foster and led him along the path. "Now, Mr. Foster, I'd like to hear your take on this orographic business and the LA scene. Plus, I'm dying to come down to Laguna Beach this summer."

"She's something, isn't she?" Kyle said as they stood alone, the rest of the party scattered here and there.

"Unique, I'd say. We don't have many Gigis where I'm from," Harriet said.

"Just spend time with my youngest sister. Ruthie's another Gigi for sure, even if she's now a wife and mother." He stood beside her, his heat coursing through her as their arms touched.

Harriet stepped away. "They're delightful."

So are you. "Yeah, they're pretty cute. Hey, wanta do something tomorrow? No pressure, just friends."

Wary, she studied his eyes in the darkness and glow of twinkle lights. "What do you have in mind?"

"Your mom says you ride. I'm a little rusty, but I did grow up on the ranch. I expect I can stay in the saddle. It's 'sposed to be a great morning. I could show you a bit of the countryside. There's a lot in bloom right now."

Harriet surprised herself by replying, "Yes, I'd love to."

"You would? Great."

She smiled. He looked like a kid in a candy store. "What time?"

"Excuse me?"

"Time? In the morning?"

"Early's probably best in case they need the horses for lessons."

"Seven?"

"Fine by me. Shall I pick you up?"

"Are we riding from Morgan's Run?"

"Yup."

"Then I'm sure I can borrow one of Spark's many vehicles. I'll find you."

At that moment, Buck Foster appeared. "Hey, Harriet, you ready?" Buck offered her his arm as Kyle tried to hide a frown.

"Of course," she said, turning to Kyle. "See you!"

Yeah, see you, he thought morosely as he watched her head off with the charming Californian. *That is if you don't ride off in the sunset with Buck Foster!*

CHAPTER 6

Harriet met Buck in the kitchen as she grabbed coffee and a bagel. "Morning!"

"Morning. It's a beauty. Where are you off to so early?"

"Kyle offered to take me riding."

"Watch out for that one. He's got his eye on you."

"Don't be ridiculous. Does not." Harriet liked Buck Foster. As a friend, like the brother she'd never had. Intuitively, she knew he wasn't trying to hit on her and he was super easy to talk to.

"Have you learned nothing, my dear? The Morgans are on the prowl day and night, married or not."

"Well, I'll have to be extra careful, won't I?" she said, waving as she grabbed a small backpack and car keys.

She drove the short distance from Spark's to Morgan's Run, Buck's teasing words echoing in her mind. *Wasn't true. He's just being friendly like the rest of his family.*

When she arrived, Kyle stood with Nick Parker, one of the wranglers. Two saddled horses stood nearby, one a gentle white Andalusian, the other a tall, chocolate Morgan.

"Hey, mornin'. Harriet, have you met Nick Parker, the ranch's horse whisperer extraordinaire?"

Harriet extended her hand. "No, hello, Mr. Parker. Harriet Winthrop. Nice to meet you."

"Likewise, Ms. Winthrop," Nick said, giving her a laconic smile. "And it's Nick."

She smiled. "Harriet, please."

Kyle watched the interplay between the two, then said, "Well, now that that's settled, meet Royal and Misty. Royal belongs to my dad, and he's gentle as a lamb, and this snow-white beauty is my mom's horse. Take your pick."

"A lady for a lady," Harriet said, patting Misty's flank. "Misty and I will do just fine."

"Good choice," Parker said as the men watched her jump onto Misty's back in one fluid motion. "I see you've done this before."

"Our friends at home run a stable in Horseshoe Crab Cove. I ride every chance I get."

Nick grinned. "Okay, then, need a leg up, Morgan?"

"Ha-ha," Kyle said as he grabbed the reins and mounted Royal. "Shall we, Ms. Winthrop?"

"Have a good ride. No hurry. We're covered for lessons."

"What's your pleasure?" he asked, drawing alongside her. "We can ride up into the foothills to the top of the east mountains and into the desert. Or we can stay in the valley and ride north along the river. There's good crossover just north of Valley Stables so we can double back and catch the west end of the Loop trail just beyond the ranch farmlands."

"The valley route sounds lovely, but you choose. Either sounds great."

"The valley it is! Up here, the trail narrows for a bit, but then it'll widen again. Follow me."

They rode for nearly thirty minutes on the narrow, winding trail, the Gila River to their left as they passed by town and plunged back into woods and scrubland. Except for a short, wider stretch near town, the path allowed only one horse at a time, so she followed Royal and Kyle, observing how comfortable and sure he was in the saddle. Despite his earlier self-deprecating remarks about being rusty,

Harriet knew few men back East who rode with the ease and confidence of Kyle Morgan. His lean, strong back was erect, and he moved as one with the horse. *They definitely do not make them like Kyle Morgan at home, that's for sure.*

Finally, they reached open pasture land, and she nudged Misty to a canter, drawing up beside Kyle and Royal.

"We almost to Valley Stables, round the next bend," he said. "Shall we let 'em go?"

She nodded.

"Yee-ha!" he cried, laughing as they flew across the open field.

Even though she was scared to death, Harriet gave Misty free rein, and she kept right up with her stable mate. Harriet held on for dear life. As they neared the edge of the field, they reined up and slowed to a trot.

He looked back at her and grinned. "That put some color in those alabaster Yankee cheeks."

She smiled. "I don't know about the alabaster, but that was pure, unbridled terror, excuse the pun."

"What, a horsewoman like you?"

"This horsewoman is used to mostly trotting or cantering, often in an indoor ring."

"That's not riding."

"Apparently not."

"Sorry if I scared you."

Harriet grinned. "I loved every second, but maybe that's enough galloping for today?"

"Done. Come on. We'll skirt the stables, then head west and cross the river. There's a nice shady spot where we can let the horses stop for a drink."

They circled the farm, then climbed until Ruthie and Harley's house came into view. They paused before reaching it, then veered west and descended the hill to the river, shallow and calm at this point. They urged the horses forward and crossed easily, then rode along the bank to a small clearing, a grove of trees providing shade.

"This is a good place to stop," he said, hopping down and coming to stand beside Misty. "Need a hand?"

"Thanks," she said, allowing him to help her down. His strong hands grasped her waist and held her as if she were a tuft of sagebrush. As she descended, she grasped his shoulders to steady herself. "Whoa, I guess I'm a little out of practice with the dismount."

"Happens to the best of us," he said, still holding her. "Okay now?"

Harriet dropped her hands, pretending to brush imaginary dust from her jeans. "Fine, thanks. You can let me go now."

He grinned, then reluctantly released her. Holding Harriet Winthrop in his arms for ten seconds had sent his libido into overdrive. He felt his cock stiffen. *Whoa, boy!* he thought, turning to guide the horses to the water.

They sat on the grassy bank, letting the horses wander along the water's edge. There wasn't a cloud in the sky, and a soft breeze whispered through the trees, blowing strands of flaxen hair across her cheeks. He reached over and tucked an errant strand behind her ear. Surprised, she turned to him. As their eyes met, a second of understanding passed between them. Despite their best efforts, there was an attraction, a raw, inescapable desire that shimmered in both their eyes. Kyle leaned forward and kissed her lightly, and she responded, parting her lips and inviting his tongue to meet hers, teasing, dancing.

However, as Kyle touched her back, drawing her closer, the spell was broken and Harriet leapt up. "No, this can't happen!" She started pacing back and forth like a caged animal. "Take me back, now! Take me back to the stables. I've got to go. Now!"

He jumped up. "Hey, hey, it's okay. I'm sorry. I was out of line. I saw something, and I thought you… Never mind that, it's okay. You're safe."

"No, I'm not! We've gotta go. Please." Not waiting for his response, she jumped onto Misty and reined her in. "Are you coming, or do I have find the way myself?"

Without a word, he mounted Royal and led the way along the bank and out of the woods to a wide open trail. "This'll take us to the crossing near the ranch's Loop Trail."

They rode at a brisk pace. Harriet stayed at least thirty feet behind him. She didn't trust herself to speak or draw any closer. His kiss had shaken her to the core. Light and tender as it had been, it had seared into her. She felt herself losing control. *He's so different from other men, and I barely know him.* She could feel the destructive urges threatening. The wish to find a dark little hole, yank at her scalp, claw her arm, binge and purge, hurting herself until the pain was so great that it obliterated the fear.

When they reached the river crossing, Kyle gazed back and saw tears streaming down her cheeks. He doubled back and came to ride beside her. "You okay?"

She nodded.

"The crossing's up ahead, but why don't we rest a minute, let you collect yourself first?"

"I'm fine. Let's go." She nudged Misty's flank and took the lead. She saw what she thought was the shallowest stretch and urged Misty into the water.

"Harriet, wait, not there!" he cried, but she ignored him and pressed forward. Suddenly, Misty whinnied as she stumbled and fell over, tossing Harriet into the cold rushing water.

CHAPTER 7

Kyle jumped from his horse and ran to them, grabbing hold of her and helping her to the bank. Misty was standing now, but in obvious distress. "You okay?" he asked, and Harriet nodded.

Kyle waded into the waist-deep water and took hold of Misty's bridle, whispering softly. "Hey, girl. Hey, let's get you out of here." Slowly, he led her to the opposite bank. As they emerged, it was obvious the horse was limping and in pain. She whinnied softly, favoring her front left leg. Kyle tied her to a tree and waded back across the narrow stretch of river to where Harriet sat on a boulder. Looks like a frightened child, he thought as he approached. "You okay?"

Harriet nodded. "What about Misty?"

"I'm not sure. Hopin' it's not broken, but I'll need to take an X-ray to be sure. Let's get you outta here now. Think you can ride?"

She nodded.

Kyle whistled for Royal, then helped Harriet into the saddle and hopped up behind her. When they reached the opposite bank, he untied Misty, and they slowly climbed to the Loop Trail.

"Should you move her?" Harriet asked, looking back at the limping horse.

"We don't have any choice. I'll tie her at the top, but we'd never get a truck down there. I'll get you back and come back with my bag to treat her."

When they reached the stables, Kyle helped her down and into her car. Harriet was shivering but refused the blanket Nick offered her. As they crossed the parking lot, two women arriving for lessons gave her quizzical looks. "Good morning!" one of them called.

Kyle nodded, then turned to Harriet. "You sure you don't want me to drive you back to Spark's? We can return the SUV later."

"Absolutely not. I'm fine, just embarrassed and worried about Misty."

"She'll be fine once we get her back here. See you this afternoon at the wedding."

"Yes," she said, turning to start the car. "I'm so sorry about Misty."

"Later," he said, tapping the car hood and heading back to the barn.

As soon as Harriet drove out, he found Nick and Jeb just heading out for lessons. "Hey, when's Maggie in?" he asked.

"A half hour or so," Jeb said. "What's up, and where's Misty?"

"Hurt, just off the Loop on the north crossover," Kyle said. "I'm gonna ride back, tape her up, and walk her back."

Nick stepped forward, handing him Royal's lead. "Jesus, what happened?"

"Stepped in a hole crossing the river," Kyle replied, bracing himself for the tirade sure to follow.

Parker frowned. "Jesus Christ, how did that happen? It's all sand. Flat as a pancake."

"Doesn't matter. It happened, and I'm going out to get her." Kyle grabbed his medical bag from the truck and stuffed it into a backpack.

Nick shook his head. "This is what happens when you let inexperienced riders out on the trails. This isn't some fancy East Coast riding barn."

"That's enough," Jeb said. "We've got lessons, Parker. Let's go."

When he reached her, Misty was standing in the shade of a small scrub pine. "Hey, girl," he said, grabbing the backpack as he slipped off Royal. He knelt beside the quivering horse and ran his fingers up and down the leg and hock, probing gently. It didn't appear broken, but a fracture was a distinct possibility. He taped the injured fetlock, which was already swollen. He didn't want to transport her.

Too unsteady. He'd have to bring the portable X-ray from Valley Stables. As Royal followed, Kyle led Misty slowly along the trail. It took them over two hours to cover the mile and a half. When they reached the barn, two of the summer workers were cleaning stalls. Kyle called for them to bring a bucket of ice, then said to Rip, "Stay with her. Ice ten minutes, off ten, then back in for ten. I'm going for a portable X-ray. Be back as soon as I can."

*****

It was three before Kyle had completed his assessment of Misty's injury. The high-quality X-ray revealed a small fracture of her long pastern bone. "Shit," he muttered when he saw the small but clear line.

Maggie sat on a stool by his side. "Bad news?"

"Small fracture. It'll probably heal up okay with six to eight weeks of box rest."

"Oh boy. She loves it outside."

"You'll need to get soft extra bedding, and I'd recommend rubber mats on the floor, especially at the door and window. I'll order some and bring 'em over. Maybe she'd play with some of the stable toys they have on the market today. Mirrors can work, and the radio. She'll need small wet feeds and plenty of water to keep her gut moving. If you can get the kids or someone to groom her twice a day, that may help with restlessness. I'll come over too."

Maggie patted his shoulder. "You have enough to do. We'll handle it. Not to worry. Care to share what happened? This isn't like Misty."

"She spooked. I spooked her."

"Misty? I'm surprised. She doesn't spook easily."

"Not Misty. Harriet. Like a dumb idiot, I kissed her, and she freaked out. Jumped on Misty and tried to cross the river upstream in the middle of the rock slide chute."

"Oh gee. We're lucky Misty didn't break her neck. I thought Harriet was an experienced rider."

"She is. Damn sight better than me, but she went completely berserk."

Maggie looked at him, eyes full of concern. "I'm sorry. Did you surprise her?"

"It was kind of spur-of-the-moment, but I thought she wanted to as much as I did. Boy, was I wrong."

"Did you apologize?"

"Abjectly, many times. I mean, she was totally freaked, Mag. I've never seen anything like it."

"Sounds like she may have had some past traumas with men."

"I felt like such a shit."

"Don't beat yourself up, sweetie," Maggie said, patting his shoulder as she stood. "Come on, we've gotta get cracking. The wedding's in an hour."

"I'm gonna stay here with Misty."

"And miss the whole thing?" she asked, eyes wide as saucers.

He grinned. "I'm probably better off here. I might get Parker to spell me after dinner just long enough to come and congratulate the newlyweds. Now you go. You've got the whole clan to get organized."

"Call us if you need help. Ben would be happy to spell you too."

"Will do. Thanks, Mag." As she vanished, he sighed. *What a day!*

CHAPTER 8

"Well, don't you ladies put the sun to shame," Spark said as Helen and Harriet appeared in the foyer. His kind eyes studied the mother and sensed something was wrong. "Can I get you anything before we head out?"

"No thanks, dear Spark," Helen said, smiling at her friend as she took his hand. It was comforting to see him after a tense few hours with her daughter. It had been a long time since she'd seen her precious child so distraught and on the edge of madness. At first, Harriet had refused to get dressed and had insisted she would not be attending the wedding. Then she began pacing the room. Helen wondered if they should put in a call to Elise, her therapist, but her daughter shook her head and said, "I can handle it, Mum. Please just give me a few minutes to shower and dress."

As Harriet pulled off her sweatshirt, Helen was relieved to see her arms were smooth and clear, no scratch marks. She had asked the housekeeper if her daughter might have a pot of hot water, and Harriet had drunk a steaming cup of an herbal tea that always calmed her. Her dress, dark green with high neck and cap sleeves, suited her even if it was, in Helen's opinion, a bit out-of-date. Harriet had never paid much attention to fashion. She wore her hair loose and pulled back with two silver combs and matching necklace and earrings of sparkling clear crystals. The effect was dazzling despite the dowdiness of her dress.

"Hello, ladies," Buck Foster said, descending behind them, looking dashing in a light gray linen suit.

"Don't they both look beautiful, son?"

Buck grinned, eyes on Harriet. "Sure do."

"Well, what're we waitin' for? Let's get this show on the road," Spark said, extending his arm to Helen as Buck did her daughter.

The ceremony was outside, on the crest of a small hill overlooking the western mountains. It was a clear, gorgeous day, not a cloud in the sky as they climbed the stone steps Spark had had installed for the wedding. He explained that post-wedding, he intended to erect a small one-room summer house with windows on all sides and screens. "It'll be kind of a retreat for me and anyone who wants to use it."

"What a lovely idea," Helen said as they climbed.

"So, how was your ride this morning?" Buck asked as they trailed behind the others.

"Fine… It was fine," she said as the elder Morgans approached with Maggie and her kids. She let go of Buck's arm and moved to stand beside Maggie.

"You okay, Harriet?" Maggie asked, blue eyes studying her.

Harriet led Maggie away from the others. "I'm fine. I've been waiting for you. How is Misty?"

Maggie leaned toward her and whispered, "We hope she'll make a full recovery, but we haven't told Leonora. Kyle wants to see how she does in the next few days."

Harriet's face fell. "Oh, I'm so sorry! It was all my fault. I feel terrible. How could I have been so foolish as to endanger that beautiful, trusting creature."

"Could have happened to any of us," Maggie said, patting her arm. "Goodness knows we've all had our reckless moments."

"It was self-centered and inexcusable," Harriet said, tears rimming her eyes.

"Hey, hey. It's okay. Please don't beat yourself up. My brother-in-law is a great vet, and my dad's with him too."

"I heard your dad was a vet."

Maggie nodded. "He never quite finished veterinary school, but he knows horses, and he's been treating Valley animals for many years."

"So they'll miss the wedding?"

Maggie smiled. "In Dad's case, that won't be a hardship. He's not a real social butterfly."

"But Kyle?"

"I dare say he'll survive. Maybe he'll pop in later. Oh my, look at this barn. Spark has outdone himself as usual, hasn't he?" Maggie gestured at the vast space festooned with flowers and candles. Twinkle lights hung everywhere—from the rafters, framing doorways, and lighting the potted trees that lined the room. The soft light revealed long tables adorned with woven strands of sagebrush, tiny air plants and seashells, some real, some silver, some sparkling crystal.

"It's magical," Harriet said, thinking she'd never seen anything like it before. "Who did the decorating?"

"Aria, his chef, brings a team from Portland to help prepare and serve. One of them, Juvana Perrault, plans all the decorations. She's pretty well known out here."

"Well, she did a wonderful job."

"Yes," Maggie said softly. "Harriet, I apologize if this is too personal, but if you ever want to talk or I can be of help, please let me know."

Harriet gazed at her with solemn eyes. "Then he told you?"

"Just a little, but as I say, we've all been there." Maggie reached out and took her hand. "I'm sorry, I see my hellion about to upset a food cart. Excuse me."

CHAPTER 9

Helen and Harriet were seated with Spark, Buck, Leonora, Ben Senior, Jeb and Amy Barnes and their son Toby. They enjoyed six courses, each complemented by a local wine. The meal began with a zesty gazpacho accompanied by a light prosecco, followed by trout poached in white wine and lemongrass, beef tenderloins served with a mushroom medley, nutty wild rice and lightly steamed asparagus, and a field greens salad with a delicate lemony dressing. Dessert was bittersweet pots au crème followed by small plates of local cheeses and fruit.

It was a simple meal, but every bite a revelation. Aria and her crew offered alternatives for people with food allergies, and there were vegetarian entrée choices.

Throughout dinner, Harriet's eyes scanned the room, but Kyle did not appear. She wondered what she'd say to him if he did, but his absence made her sad and anxious. As the band began playing Whitney Houston's "I Will Always Love You," Kevin led Polly to the dance floor. They looked so happy and peaceful, Harriet smiled. *That's what love looks like*, she mused.

She turned away to take a sip of wine and spied Kyle at the barn doorway chatting with his brother Sam. Both brothers looked handsome in dark suits, almost like twins, although Kyle was shorter. Without realizing it, she let out a deep, audible sigh. This attracted the notice of both her mother and Buck, who turned to stare at her. Harriet shook her head, then stood. "Excuse me," she said to Amy, who sat beside her. "Time for a trip to the ladies' room."

"You know where they are?" Amy asked. When Harriet shook her head, Spark's daughter pointed to the far end of the room. "Just beyond the grove of ficus."

"Thanks," Harriet said, hurrying off, certain her face was as red as a beet.

After emerging from the bathroom, she hung back in the shadows, scanning the room. Finally, she spotted Kyle at one of the bars, chatting with Kevin's coworkers. As she watched, he raised his beer, then turned away from the room, dark eyes searching. When their eyes met, he smiled. Harriet's chest constricted, the shame of her foolish actions washing over her. Not only had she been responsible for injuring an innocent animal, she had now prevented Kyle from attending the wedding. *He should be here, not me!*

She was as attracted to him as he was to her. *This is a major problem.* Light-headed and queasy from all the wine, she grabbed a bottle of water from one of the colorful baskets near the restrooms and took a few sips. When she turned back, she couldn't see him.

"Hey," a voice said to her left.

Harriet jumped. "Oh!"

"Sorry, didn't mean to startle you," Kyle said. "I can't stay long, but wanted to say hi. Don't 'spose you'd like to dance?"

"Yes, yes, I would." She set down the water and offered him her hand.

Surprised, he took it gently and led her through the gyrating crowd. As the band finished Van Halen's "Jump" and began playing Alicia Keys "That's How Strong My Love Is," Kyle turned and drew her into his arms. His warm smile made tears spring to her eyes.

"Hey, I'm not that bad, am I?"

"No, I'm just… I'm so very sorry about this morning and Misty and everything. How is she?"

"Ned Williams and I have been checking in her. He's our local vet, Maggie's dad."

Harriet nodded.

"We both agree that she has a good chance of a full recovery. Next week, we'll have a better idea."

"I wish it was my leg. I feel so terrible. Is it broken?"

"Small fracture."

In an uncharacteristic move, she buried her head against his chest. "Oh, Kyle, I am so, so sorry for Misty and for the way I behaved."

He moved away slightly, dropped her hand, and cupped her chin. He had gentle hands. Healing hands. "Hey, hey, all's well, babe. Misty's a strong girl, and I'm impulsive. What can I say? A beautiful woman turned my head."

When Harriet looked up, he was grinning the trademark Morgan grin that turned women's knees to jelly and their hearts to mush. "Thank you for saying that."

"It's true," he said, taking her hand again. "Now, let's dance, 'cause I've gotta get back and relieve Ned."

As he pulled her closer, Harriet was afraid to breathe. "Can I come with you?"

He gazed down, studying her for a few seconds. "If you really want to, but this is a great party Spark's got goin' here."

"I'm not much of a party girl, and besides, *you* should be here, not me."

"You look really pretty, by the way. We don't see that style out here much."

She smiled. "That's because it hasn't been in fashion since the Civil War. I'm not much of a dresser. My sisters are always teasing me about being old-fashioned."

"Well, you look just fine to me." He leaned in, and his lips grazed her forehead, a brotherly kiss. As they moved to the music, Kyle felt himself growing hard despite his best efforts to squelch his treacherous libido. Old-fashioned or not, there was something about the woman he held in his arms. Something smoldering and hot that awakened feelings he didn't even know he had.

The music ended, and Harriet sighed, hating to step away. Just before Kyle pulled back, she felt his erection, and a shiver of desire shot up her spine. "That was nice."

"Yes, it was, but I've gotta go. You sure you want to come?"

"Please, yes. Can you give me five minutes to run in the house and change? Could I meet you at your truck, or should I ask to borrow one of Spark's cars?"

"I can take you. Go. Take ten. I'll say my goodbyes to the newlyweds and meet you out there. I'm parked behind the catering vans."

Harriet hurried off, finding her mother with Leonora. It appeared that deceit was her only option. She told them she had a headache and was going to call it a night. Helen had observed the dance. She studied her daughter, who did not appear to be the slightest bit ill. "Oh, I'm sorry, sweetheart. Shall I come with you?"

"No, I'm just going to bed. Please congratulate Polly and Kevin again for me."

Leonora's arm circled her waist. "Now, darlin', we've got a couple of doctors here. Can one of them take a peek at you?"

"Absolutely not. Just a long day and too much wine," Harriet said as she inched away from the pair. "Night, ladies!"

"Night, ladies, indeed," Leonora said as they watched Harriet hurry across the room and out of the barn. "I saw them too, and I know my son. You wait, he'll disappear momentarily."

Helen smiled at her friend. Sure enough, at that moment, they spied Kyle Morgan at the barn door saying his goodbyes.

CHAPTER 10

Horses nickered softly as they walked through the darkened barn toward the light. When they reached Misty's stall, Ned was sitting on a stool in the dark, observing her. "How's she doin'?" Kyle asked, unsuccessful in affecting a nonchalant tone. He was worried, and so was the tall, wiry wrangler who rose as they entered.

"Pretty good," Ned said. "She's calm. Tried to get her to lie down, but she won't do it. Never been happy on the ground, so I doubt we'll coax her to do it now. Maybe in a couple of days."

"I've been thinking that we could rig up a sling," Kyle said, gazing up at the rafters. "Not so she's off the ground, but lifted enough to take most of the weight off."

Ned raised his eyes but said nothing.

"I saw it done once during my residency. It was pretty effective for a short time."

"Got one handy?" Ned said.

"No, but I'll bet between what we've got here and at Valley Stables, we can rig something up. Let me research a little bit."

Ned nodded, then smiled at Harriet, who had been listening from the doorway. "Evenin', miss."

"Oh shit, I'm sorry!" Kyle said. "No manners. Ned Williams, this is Harriet Winthrop, Helen's daughter."

"Pleased to meet you, Ms. Winthrop," Ned said, extending his hand, which Harriet took.

"And, it's Harriet, please. You've probably heard that I'm the one responsible for poor Misty's injury. I couldn't be sorrier."

"Happens to the best of us," Ned said, his eyes warm. "Goodness knows some of my rides took a beating in the old days."

"Ned's the Valley's most famous wrangler," Kyle said. "They tell many a story about him at the local watering holes."

Ned chuckled. "All bad, I'm sure."

"You go ahead home, Ned. I'll stay with her," Kyle said.

"You sure? I'm retired with lots of time. Won't they need you out at the stables early tomorrow?"

"My assistant's there. It'll be fine."

"Well then, I'll head out," he said, grabbing a leather case. "Harriet, it was a pleasure."

Ned disappeared, leaving them alone in the stillness of the barn, the silence broken by the occasional hoot of an owl or howl of a coyote.

CHAPTER 11

After Ned's departure, Harriet paced the stall, stopping to stroke Misty's flank from time to time. Kyle watched but said nothing. Fifteen minutes elapsed before he stood and left, returning shortly with a second stool. "You may want this at some point."

"I'm acting like a crazy person, aren't I?"

"No."

"I do this to forestall the rest."

"It's okay by me," he said, kind eyes regarding her. Harriet had changed into jeans, a T-shirt, and worn running shoes. Her flaxen hair was tied back in a loose ponytail, and she had removed what little makeup she had applied for the wedding. *Never lovelier*, he thought, watching her. *Fragile and beautiful. Like a wounded bird.*

"Maybe I should sneak back to Spark's and get snacks. Did you even have dinner?" Harriet asked.

"I'm fine. There are drinks and snacks in the office."

"I'm doing this because I'd like to explain, and I'm screwing up the courage."

"Harriet, don't push to say anything on my account. Please. I've been in dark places. It sucks. You're with a friend here. Take care of *you* and don't worry about me."

She stopped in front of him and, to his surprise, flopped down in a pile of clean hay and buried her head in her hands. "What a mess I am!"

"How 'bout a beer, or seltzer or whatever's in the fridge?" he said. "Maybe a snack? Then together we can untangle the mess?"

She lifted her head slightly, giving him a wan smile. "I'd love a beer, but I fear it won't help."

When Kyle returned, he found her lying back on a hay bale, her eyes closed. As he sat, she opened her eyes and brushed hay from her head and body. "I'm assuming you have an outhouse or something here?"

He laughed. "This is a modern facility. Bathroom's end of the hall to the right. Light is a string hanging in the middle of the room. Wave your arms. You'll grab hold of it. Want me to come show you?"

"Sit, please. I can wave my arms as maniacally as the next person. Be right back."

When she returned, he'd settled in a pile of soft hay close to the wall and was leaning back, watching Misty. As she sat beside him, he handed her a bottle. "Desert Amber, our local brew. It's actually pretty good."

"Thanks," she said, leaning against the rough wood wall. Misty nickered softly, then closed her eyes. "Is that how she sleeps?"

"Most of the time. I'd say she lies down for some good REM sleep about one night a week."

"Is that normal?"

"For her, yes. No one watches her twenty-four seven, so she might sneak some lie-down time when the barn's quiet."

"She's a beauty."

"Yup. My dad's gift to Mom on their twenty-fifth anniversary. That would be when Mom expressed interest in riding for about ten seconds. Mostly, Misty's a stable horse. Steady and great for lessons and pack trips. She's a good girl."

"Yes, she is," Harriet said, her eyes sad as she gazed at the white Andalusian.

"She's gonna be fine. I have a good feeling about it. Ned too. Tell me more about back home and where you learned to ride so well."

"Not well enough, as it turns out," she said. "There's a farm and stables in the Cove, not far from where Mom lives. We summered in the Cove, Horseshoe Crab Cove, to be exact. My mom's friend Faith and her husband run the farm now, and their daughter Karen is my dearest friend. I worked part-time there during the summer months. Even stayed on a little longer a couple of times to stay out of the house. My dad was not a nice person in those days. It was a horror show, especially for my mom."

Harriet's left hand trembled, and she brought it continually to her opposite wrist, clawlike, as if she meant to begin scratching. Finally, she set her beer down and clasped her hands together, white knuckled.

"You okay?" he said softly.

She nodded. "Just trying to avoid bad habits."

Kyle waited.

"I used to hurt myself. Scratch my wrists till they bled, starve myself, binge, purge. You name it, I did it."

"Must've been really hard."

She shrugged. "I spent my childhood hiding in a closet, if that explains anything. A lot of the time, Mom was in there with me, trying to coax me out."

"You must be an incredibly strong person."

"My mom's the strong one. I was the invisible child who survived by doing nothing."

He reached over and took her hand. She was trembling, but didn't pull away. "But you survived. That's huge," he said softly.

Harriet leaned against his shoulder. "Would it be okay if I just rested here a minute? I'm suddenly feeling really sleepy."

"Be my guest." Kyle was afraid to breathe in case he spooked her. "Horseshoe Crab Cove, huh?"

She nodded. "Living in the village saved my mom's life. She has a group of wonderful women who call themselves the Darn Yarners. They've been such a huge source of love and support for her, especially since the death of her second husband, Tim."

"Darn Yarners? Knitters?"

Harriet chuckled. "It started as a book club and evolved into storytelling, poetry readings, whatever they came up with. I haven't seen my mother pick up knitting needles yet, but you never know."

"Tell me more about these yarners," he said, loving the feel of her body against his.

"There are eight of them including my mom. She and another of the yarners, Frankie, met 'cause they both do stained glass work, although Mom's slowed down a lot in that department. Has to be a very big or very special client for her to take a job these days."

Kyle nodded, "That's how our two mothers met, when Helen did windows for our grandparents."

"I've seen pictures of those windows. Your grandfather was some kind of Hollywood celebrity, wasn't he?" she asked, yawning sleepily.

"He was an agent to several major celebrities, and my grandmother was one of those people you read about on the society pages. She apparently gave amazing parties."

"That must have been quite a life. Did you spend much time out there?"

"No, we never knew our grandparents. They died in a plane crash shortly after our parents' marriage, of which they did not approve."

"Why not?" she asked, her voice heavy with sleep. "Your dad's terrific."

"To them, he was a farmer. His parents had all this land in the Valley, but they lived in a ramshackle old farmhouse, now transformed into my brother and Maggie's dream house that I showed you. The story goes that the pre-wedding visit to the Valley by Mom and her folks did not go well. I believe the words hick, hayseed, and others were thrown around on the drive back to LA. But Mom was unmoved. She was crazy in love with Dad then and still is."

"Lucky...so lucky," Harriet murmured as her head sank deeper against his chest and her breath softened.

Kyle smiled, leaning back and getting comfortable. "You sleep, baby," he said aloud. *I could hold you like this forever.*

CHAPTER 12

"Well, this is a cozy sight," Ben Morgan said, standing beside Maggie and Nick as Ned Williams quietly examined Misty's leg.

Jeb Barnes, her assistant, came to peer into the stall as Maggie gave her husband an elbow. "Shh! You'll wake them up," she whispered.

Nick pushed back his hat and grinned. "Gonna have to wake 'em up soon. Lessons'll be starting."

Maggie shook her head. "Poor babies, they must've stayed up all night with Misty."

"Poor babies! Spark's probably got half the county out looking for that baby," her husband said. "Probably wanna take a buggy whip to my poor baby brother."

"I can hear you," Kyle said, raising the hat he had over his face. "Hope you're all having fun."

As he stirred, Harriet woke with a start. "Oh! Oh my goodness!" She sat up, brushing hay from her jeans.

Ned rose and stepped out of the stall as Maggie closed the door and shooed the others along. "Come on cowboys. There's work to do around here, you know. Let's give them a few minutes privacy."

*****

"So tell me more about those yarners," Kyle said as they settled into a booth at Gracie's.

"I'm still too mortified to think straight," Harriet said. "Have I still got hay in my hair?"

He grinned, his dark eyes dancing with light. "Looks pretty clean from here. And there's no need to be mortified or embarrassed. This *is* the Wild West, you know."

"That doesn't mean I should go wild. Do you think I might have had too much to drink? What must your family think of me! And Spark!"

"Harriet, really. Don't sweat it. My family's cool and Spark too. Did you speak to your mom?"

"Yes, and she seemed remarkably calm about the whole thing."

"That's because we're adults, not a couple of crazy teenagers. And we were takin' care of a horse, not having a drunken orgy. It happens out here."

Harriet's face fell. "What about your mom? Did you tell her about Misty?"

"No, Ben told her it was one of the mustangs. She's too busy with the Cowbelles and the fair next week to think twice about it. Now tell me about your yarners. You nodded off at the good part."

Harriet laughed. "I doubt that."

"Mornin', kids," Gracie said, pad in hand, apron already streaked with what looked like blueberry syrup. "What'll you have?"

They both ordered omelets, and Gracie disappeared into the kitchen as Maria, her regular waitress, came out with a fresh pot of coffee. Once she'd poured theirs and asked if they needed anything, they were left alone. The diner was unusually quiet. Only a few booths were occupied, and several people sat at the counter.

Harriet sipped the strong, excellent coffee and sighed. "So...the yarners. Where did I leave off?"

"You'd started talking about your mom and her stained glass buddy."

"Frankie, yes. She's a hoot. Her main job is private investigating. Frankie's divorced, no kids. Then there's Rosa. She and her husband, Cesar, run the best restaurant in town.

"Horseshoe Crab Cove is on the Atlantic Flyway. The migratory birds are incredible, so we get a lot of ornithologists out there. There's also a small research facility collecting data on the town's namesake. Horseshoe crabs are part of a delicate ecosystem that, like everything else, is being threatened. Belle, Mom's friend and fellow yarner, runs the lab with her husband and two sons.

"Mavis is the most flamboyant yarner. She's an event planner. Small as Mom's town is, the peninsula that comprises more than half of it is a really popular wedding destination. Lots of gorgeous waterfront property, vineyards, open fields, stonewalls. Horseshoe Crab Cove Winery is part of a huge farm owned by another yarner, Faith Newbury and her husband. Their parents and grandparents owned the largest tract of land on the peninsula, and they have an amazing organic farm. Not as big as yours, but it's been really successful, and the vineyard too. Different family members run each. They also have a small stable that my friend Karen owns, where they board horses, give lessons, and run summer pony camps."

"Sounds like this place," he said, nodding as Maria set down their plates.

"In miniature," she said. "Faith has two sisters, also yarners, Grace and Hope. Hope runs a spa and yoga center and Grace and her family run the docks and fishery. So there you have it—the yarners all—Mom, Frankie, Belle, Rosa, Mavis, Faith, Hope and Grace. They're an amazing group of women, most of whom have known each other their whole life. Mom's the latecomer but has been with the yarners since she moved to the Cove."

"Cool."

"It is pretty cool. They've been wonderful role models."

"No second-generation yarners?"

Harriet laughed. "We're always welcome, but so far, no. They meet once a month or so. Depending upon what they're up to for the year, they might meet more often. Some of my generation goes occasionally. Lucy, my sister, attends 'cause her schedule's more flexible and her business is right in town."

"So she lives in town?"

"No, about twenty minutes south. This omelet is incredible, by the way. Thank you for suggesting this. I feel much better with food and coffee."

"I'm glad." Kyle wanted to reach across the table and take her hand, but held back, afraid he'd spook her.

It had been a long time since he'd enjoyed a woman's company as he did Harriet's. Aside from the smoldering attraction he was trying to ignore, there was a fragile quiet to Harriet that touched his heart. When their eyes met, he was lost. Gonzo. Beyond smitten. *She's not even my type.* His type were usually blonde, curvaceous, and sexy. Devil-may-care women who wanted a fun night with zero strings. He had dated a few women for longer stretches in college and vet school, but he was mostly a love-'em-and-leave-'em guy. Just like his older brother Ben had been until Maggie Williams came along. *This doesn't feel like love 'em and leave 'em.* He wasn't at all sure what to do. *Enjoy it, buddy.*

As he pulled up to Spark's an hour later, Kyle said, "You doin' okay?"

Harriet flashed a shy smile. "Aside from being desperately in need of a shower, yes. I'm doing fine. Thanks for bringing me home." She grasped the door handle.

"Harriet?"

"Yes?"

"I don't want to push my luck or rattle you, but I really enjoy your company. I don't 'spose you'd like to do something tonight or tomorrow? I'm not even sure how long you're staying."

"At least another week, unless Mum asks to extend a bit."

"So? What d'ya think? Are you willing to risk another get-together? Notice I'm not calling it a date."

"Thank you for that. And, yes, I'd like that. I'm not sure what Spark and Mom have in mind for me today."

"I've gotta get to work, but I'll call around noon. Does that sound okay?"

"Yes, that would be great." She smiled as she turned to open the door. "Bye."

Kyle waved as he drove down the drive. *I don't know if you can keep this going, buddy, but she's sure worth a try!*

CHAPTER 13

Harriet slipped through Spark's front door, hoping to avoid the third degree until she had showered and changed. No such luck. Helen called from the breakfast room before her foot hit the stairs. "Morning, honey! Everything okay?"

Harriet veered right and was relieved to find her mother alone in the light-filled room, its colorful wallpaper reflecting the greenery that thrived inside and out. For the hundredth time, Harriet marveled at the decorating genius behind this extraordinary house. She bent and kissed her mother's cheek. "Morning, Mum. I really need a shower."

Helen smiled. "I should say so, after a night in a horse stall."

"How did you know?"

"Valley grapevine. There aren't many secrets here. Sit for just a minute." Helen patted the chair beside her.

"Where's Spark?"

"Off to Valley Stables. They've got horses arriving today, and workers too, I think."

"You look very comfy in your robe and slippers."

Helen sighed, leaning back in her chair. "This is the life, isn't it? Slow and relaxing. Of course, it doesn't hurt to be living in the lap of luxury and being waited on hand and foot. Want coffee or something to eat?"

"I'm good, thanks."

"Gracie's is very filling."

Harriet laughed, throwing up her hands. "I give up! Which omelet did I order?"

"Never mind that. Tell me about your night."

"There's nothing to tell. We were watching Misty, sitting in her stall, and fell asleep. Sleeping, nothing else. When we woke up, half the town was standing over us. Very embarrassing. Then Kyle took me to breakfast, and here I am, smelling like hay and horse manure."

"He's a nice boy."

"*Man*, Mother. Younger than me, but still a man."

"Not that much younger."

"Six years. He's twenty-nine, and I'm thirty-five."

"That's nothing."

"Mother, we're friends. I'm not looking for a relationship as you well know. He's a nice man and the Morgans are great, but my life is back East and my heart is not ready for anything more after you-know-who." Harriet rarely spoke Louis's name and had forbidden her sisters and mother to do so.

Helen reached for her hand. "You know, sweetheart, opening your heart to a kind man and a loving family is not the same as... Well it's not the same as your college experience. Not all men are like him or your dad during his dark period."

"I know, but I haven't hurt myself for nearly ten years. I can't risk it."

"Okay," Helen said, patting her hand. "You're the boss. You can have fun as friends, though, right?"

Harriet raised her eyebrow, giving her mother a look. "Yes, we can. Actually, in that vein, we may do something tonight, unless you need me."

"I believe Spark and I are dining at the Club with Leonora and Ben. They invited you too, of course. I'm sure they won't be offended if you beg out."

"Give you all a chance to mobilize your spies to trail us tonight. Right?"

"Ha-ha, now run along and take that shower. I think I'm getting a whiff of manure."

Harriet jumped up.

Helen watched as she almost skipped out of the room and thought she hadn't ever seen her daughter this happy.

As soon as she closed the bedroom door, Harriet called Kyle's cell. *A friendly call*, she told herself, *but isn't it fun?*

"Hey," he said, answering on the first ring.

"It's me, Harriet. Turns out I am free tonight, if you'd still like to do something?"

"Great. I'll pick you up at seven. Does that work?"

"Yes. Where are we going? What should I wear?"

"It's a surprise, but dress casual. No riding. No horse barn."

"Okay, see you then."

"Looking forward to it," he said, ringing off.

He still had a big shit-eating grin on his face as he bumped into Harley. "Hey, buddy, you look like a pig in shit," his boss said, eyeing him.

"Great shit," Kyle said.

"Hot date?"

"Something like that."

"If it's Helen's daughter, she's a beauty."

"Yes, she is."

"You ready for the truck? Should be here in a half hour or so."

"We'll be ready," Kyle said as Harley tipped his hat and disappeared into the barn.

*****

After showering, Harriet wandered downstairs and found her mother preparing to go out. "I'm going to walk Spark's new trail that rings the property. It's about a mile and a half. I may do it twice depending upon how I'm feeling. Would you like to come along?"

"Thanks, but I'm going to grab a book and sit on the sunporch. I'll take a run later."

Harriet watched her mother sally forth, then headed to Spark's library. Surely she could find something in his vast collection that would help while away a few hours. After orienting herself, she browsed his fiction section and selected a Willa Cather that she'd never read. Book under her arm, she headed for the kitchen to get a glass of water, surprised to find Aria Firorelli sitting at one of the room's three marble-topped islands, crying as she chopped vegetables.

"I don't see any onions," Harriet said softly. "Are you okay?"

"Oh, sure, just dandy. My crew left this morning, and here I am. Once again, alone, in this huge place. I love Spark and would follow him to the ends of the earth, but I'm so sick of having no friends here."

Harriet drew up a stool and sat beside the raven-haired chef. "I know we're strangers, but I'm a good listener. I also get where you're coming from."

Aria gave her a glazed look, her violet eyes rimmed with tears, then shrugged. "Why not? Welcome to old boys' heaven, where the cowboys are gorgeous, hot, and either married or gay."

Harriet smiled. "Surely there are a few still single?"

"No one who's interested in me."

"I can't believe that," Harriet said. "You're beautiful and incredibly talented."

"Culinary tastes around here tend toward chuck wagon fare."

Harriet chuckled. "What about women friends?"

"It's tough, you know? I mean the Morgans and Spark's family are great people, but they're a pretty close-knit group, and the women are either working or moms or members of the Cowbelles. There never seems to be a good time to hang out, you know? It's not like Portland. There's no night life to speak of except the Bulldog. Talk about cowboy heaven! Have you been there?"

"No, not yet. Doesn't sound like my mother's type of place."

"Food's not bad. They get sandwiches for the lunch crowd from the café, and Russ Keeler makes a mean Bulldog Burger."

Harriet grinned. "I do love a good burger once in a while."

"Would you like some iced tea?"

"I'd love some."

Aria grabbed a tissue on her way to one of several refrigerators. She brought two glasses of tea, a plate of lemons, and a small vase holding sprigs of mint. "Do you use sweetener? I have sugar, Stevia, monk fruit, and honey."

"I'm fine, thanks. Monk fruit?"

"It's Spark's favorite. He's got a major sweet tooth, but he's not supposed to have sugar. This is the most like it," she said, showing Harriet a small sugar bowl filled with what looked like sugar. "Feel free to try it. It's pretty tasty."

Harriet put a small taste on her palm and licked. "Ooh, that is good. Where do you get it?"

"I buy it online, but I think you could probably find it in Tucson and maybe at SD. Have you been there yet?"

Harriet shook her head.

"SD stands for Saguaro Dreams. It's a three-story emporium in town that has a little bit of everything. They have a pretty big health food section. I'd check it out while you're here. It's pretty amazing. Lots of local art. Hope Seymour hangs a few of her paintings there."

"I'd love to. You wouldn't be free anytime today and like to go with me? Maybe a late lunch at the Bulldog?"

"You mean it?"

"Of course. I don't know people here either, so we can navigate cowboy town together."

"I could be ready to go in an hour. Just a little work to do, then I'll clean up."

"Great. I'll be in the sunroom pretending I'm mistress of the manor. Come get me when you're ready," Harriet said, raising her glass in a mock toast.

*****

Harriet and Aria spent an hour browsing the three floors of Saguaro Dreams, or SD, as the locals called it. Harriet purchased some small gifts for her family and her house sitter. As they strolled through the women's clothing section, Aria found a flowing purple kimono, which she intended to use as a swimsuit cover-up. "What do you think?" she asked Harriet.

"Lovely. It brings out the color of your beautiful eyes."

"Liz Taylor eyes, my mother calls them."

"She's right. You'll look more amazing than Liz lolling around Spark's pool."

"Not that there's anyone there to notice me."

"What about Buck?"

Aria crinkled her nose and made a face. "He couldn't be less interested. Believe me, I've been chasing him since I started working for Spark."

Harriet smiled. "I'd buy it. You never know who might come along!"

Aria chuckled. "Yeah, right. Okay, I'll get it. Now let's find something for *you*!"

After Aria talked her into getting a similar kimono in deep greens and reds, they headed for the gallery on the first floor. They stood for a long time gazing at one of Hope's paintings, a landscape that looked vaguely familiar.

"She's mega talented, isn't she?" Aria said.

"Sure is. This is remarkably similar to the one that hangs in Spark's great room, isn't it?"

"Same westward view, slightly farther south. I'm gonna guess this was painted at Ben and Maggie's or right around there. Have you seen their place?"

"Kyle drove me by. Mom and I are going to lunch there sometime this week, I think," Harriet said.

"It's spectacular. I mean, Ruthie and Harley's house is amazing, not to mention Lang and Beth's, and of course Spark's and the Morgans' homes are none too shabby. But if I had my choice, I'd live at Ben and Maggie's dream house. So romantic how Ben and his brother designed and had it built as a surprise. Maggie's one lucky woman."

"From what I know of her, Ben's pretty lucky too," Harriet said.

"Yup, Saguaro's beautiful couple. That's what people call them. Come on, I'm getting hungry."

CHAPTER 14

"You grab a booth, and I'll order two Bulldog burgers," Aria said as they stepped into the dark, wood-paneled saloon. Almost one now, the lunch crowd was dwindling. A few patrons sat at the bar, and half the booths were occupied.

As Harriet headed toward an empty booth, Kyle stepped out of the kitchen laden with bags and crashed into her. "Harriet? Hey, sorry. You okay? Grabbin' a late lunch for the crew." A pretty brunette followed him, laden with bags as well. "This is Patty Turner, my assistant. Can't remember, have you guys met? Patty, this is Harriet Winthrop, daughter of a friend of Spark's."

"Hi," Harriet sputtered. "So good to meet you,"

"Hi, glad to meet you too. Sorry I can't shake hands," Patty said. "Gotta get these back to a hungry crew." Patty looked neither sorry nor glad to meet her.

"You here alone?" Kyle asked, gazing around.

"No, Aria and I are having lunch."

He leaned toward her and whispered, "Whip Woman? How'd that happen?"

"Shh," Harriet said. "We've been having a great time."

A frown creased Patty's pale brow, and she appeared to have a proprietary interest in her boss. Harriet guessed her to be mid-twenties, with pale alabaster skin, straight dark shoulder-length hair, and a petite figure.

Aria approached the group. "Hey, Morgan," she said, nodding.

Kyle grinned. "Hey, Aria. Can't remember. Have you met Patty?"

"Yup."

An awkward silence followed until Kyle said, "Well, we'd better get movin'. See you, ladies."

Aria rolled her eyes as they watched the two depart. "See what I mean? He's clearly into you, and Ms. Stick-Up-Her-Ass is none too happy about it."

Harriet laughed. "Come on, we're back here."

They had a lively lunch, each woman recounting some of her past. Aria appeared to have been as unlucky in love as Harriet had, albeit not taken to the cleaners. "What a bastard," she said as Harriet described the disaster that had befallen her with Louis and his conniving partner. "Is he in jail?"

Harriet shook her head. "They disappeared. There are still warrants out, but it's been almost fourteen years. Not much chance of finding them or the money now."

"I'm really sorry," Aria said, her violet eyes soft and warm as she gazed at Harriet.

"Thanks. It's been a long haul."

"I guess. I mean I've dated some losers and assholes, but nothing like that. You're an incredibly strong woman."

"Years of therapy and hospitalizations got me here. I was pretty messed up from childhood even before the college stuff. I was hurting myself in so many ways. Scratching my arms till they bled, starving myself, binging, purging. I was a horror show."

"Geez, sweetie, how'd you get out of it?"

"My mom and sisters. They had me hospitalized and found me a wonderful therapist. Elise literally saved my life."

"You're lucky. I have one sister, and she's a complete flake. My mom's okay. She's on her fourth husband, and he's definitely her focus. Not a bad guy in comparison to the other losers she's hooked up with. My dad left when I was two, but he was no loss. Alcoholic abuser."

"Mine too," Harriet said quietly.

Aria gazed up, a look of surprise on her face. "Really?"

Harriet nodded. "My downward spiral started long before college. I spent three-quarters of my childhood in a coat closet. My mom was often right there with me."

"Geez, honey."

"Yeah, a story for another day. My stomach's about to burst. That burger was delicious. I can't believe I ate the whole thing."

"I can't believe the connections," Aria said, gesturing from Harriet to herself.

Harriet smiled, patting her hand. "So I guess it's good that we found each other. I'm thinking I should get back, though."

"Me too. Harriet?"

"Yeah?"

"Thanks. Today was really fun."

"For me too," she said as they strolled to the bar to pay the tab.

On the way to the car, Aria turned to her. "Next time, we're gonna start plotting my search for a man *and* we're gonna zero in on strategies for you and Mr. Hunky Veterinarian."

Harriet laughed. "We're just friends!"

"Yeah, right, and I'm Cinder-frickin'-rella!"

CHAPTER 15

Even though Kyle said to be casual, Harriet chose her wardrobe carefully. She wore her favorite jeans that she knew fit her body like a glove, and a light azure top that brought out the color in her eyes and hugged her full round breasts just enough without seeming slutty. Her sister Hazel called it her *"boob shirt, but a nice-girl boob shirt."* Harriet smiled, thinking of her youngest sister. She missed her. When she got home, they would definitely plan a weekend visit.

Her hair fell in loose waves framing her oval face. At the last minute, she decided to add a thin headband. Tiny silver earrings were her only jewelry. They sparkled as she gazed in the mirror.

"This will have to do," she said aloud, "but at least I feel comfortable." Kyle's expression when he saw her let her know that she'd chosen well.

"Hey, you look great," he said, waving at Spark and Helen, who sat on the terrace, drinks in hand.

Harriet smiled. Kyle wore jeans and a ranch T-shirt, but unlike most Valley men, he was in hiking shoes, not cowboy boots. *Good enough to eat* came to mind before Harriet banished the thought. "You don't look too shabby yourself, Dr. Morgan."

He laughed. "Don't hear that much from my patients, or anyone else, for that matter. The doctor part, I mean. You all set?"

"Am I okay? I brought a sweater, just in case."

"You're perfect. Sweater's a good idea. Let's go."

When she slid into the truck, he handed her a bag. "For you. Put one on each wrist and ankle."

"Excuse me?"

"They're for bugs. Mosquitos, mostly. They're safe. My brother-in-law Lang's company, Rambler Sports, sells them. They work great. Healthier and much more effective than any spray or cream."

As she unwrapped the brightly colored stretchy rings, she said, "So what you're telling me is we're headed for a bog or swamp?"

"Not exactly. We might get lucky and be bug-free, but better safe than sorry."

"Where are we going, anyway?"

"To one of my favorite spots in the valley." They drove through town and took a dirt road that ran along the Gila River. After several miles, he pulled over. "It's about a ten-minute walk. Are you okay with that?"

"I guess I better be," she said, hopping out.

Kyle grabbed a backpack from the truck bed. "Dinner," he said. The pack looked heavy, and a red blanket was rolled and strapped to its top.

"You cook?"

"I do, actually, but this is Carmela's food. Always great, whereas mine tends toward the experimental. Moments of greatness mixed with disaster and mediocrity. Carm's never made a bad meal in her life. Ready?"

He took her hand and guided her toward a trail that led into the woods. His touch was warm, and Harriet felt her body responding as he led them upward. As the path narrowed, he dropped her hand. She felt instantly cold and bereft, craving the strength of his touch. She sighed, breathing deeply. *He is a friend, Harriet Winthrop. Nothing more!*

After ten minutes of climbing, the trail widened, and she realized they had reached the top of a ridge. Boulders and outcroppings surrounded them, but there was a grassy area inside what looked like a giant stone bowl. He turned back to her, arms wide, huge grin. "This is Craggy Bowl. Pretty cool. Huh?"

"Very cool. How did it get here?"

"Mother Nature, I guess. My brother Robbie and I discovered it on a camping trip. We swore never to tell another soul. I'm not sure if he ever comes up here, but I do, from time to time, when I want to think. It's my spiritual place."

"It's beautiful and so peaceful."

He nodded. "I suspect many people have their favorite spot in this valley of ours. This is one of mine."

"It's that way at home too. People find their spot and keep it a secret."

"I've never shared this secret with anyone," he said softly.

Harriet met his eyes and glimpsed sadness in their dark, warm depths. She took a deep breath, relieved that she hadn't said something flippant like *I bet you take all your ladies here.*

"Thank you for sharing it with me."

He grinned, the wolfish Morgan men's smile, and shook out the blanket. "My pleasure. Now let's see what Carm has packed for us."

Moment passed, Harriet thought, helping to spread the blanket. But there had been a moment. She was certain of it.

CHAPTER 16

"Dessert is lace cookies. They're pretty spectacular," Kyle said, pulling a small tin from the pack. "She may have put some raspberries in too. She knows they're my favorite."

"Oh my goodness, I don't think I can eat another bite!" Harriet said. "It was all incredible. I can't even imagine the luxury of having my own chef."

"That's my parents' world, and Sparks, of course. The rest of us fend for ourselves. Not sure what Mom and Dad will do if Carmela retires. Mom can cook, but she's had Carmela practically her whole life."

"She's seems like a wonderful person."

"She is. Like a second mom. Here." He held out a lacy oatmeal cookie that appeared to be infused with chocolate.

Harriet leaned forward, and his fingers grazed her chin as she took a small bite. "Oh my, that is good."

He smiled, holding out the cookie. "See? I bet you want the rest, right?"

Harriet laughed. "Yes, as a matter of fact, I do."

Feeling bold after two glasses of excellent chardonnay, she finished her cookie, chose another, and said, "So why did you decide to share this special place with me?"

If the question surprised him, Kyle didn't let on. Without hesitation, he said, "'Cause you're special. I mean you're a special person, and you're also special to me."

She gazed into his eyes and saw sincerity. "This is dangerous territory for me, Kyle."

"I know," he said quietly. "Please don't push yourself."

"I mean, I want to…but I'm scared to death."

"I know, so just enjoy the night and nothing more. I'm just happy spending time with you."

"Why?"

"Because I like you, and I've never met anyone quite like you before."

Tears sprang to her eyes, and she looked away. "I'm such a train wreck."

"Hey, hey, don't go there," he said, taking her hand.

"But I want to. My whole body wants to go there."

He grinned, patting her hand, then releasing it. "Confession? Mine too, but I don't want to spoil the moment." *I've never wanted any woman like I want you, Harriet Winthrop.*

"But I'm older than you. By a lot."

"Matters not a bit."

"And we barely know each other."

"You're right about that," he said, willing his voice to stay soft and neutral. *Don't scare her!*

"Can I?" she asked, leaning toward him, kissing him softly. He responded, and she pulled back. "I was going to say, can I kiss you?"

He smiled. "I got that. It was nice."

"Can I do it again?"

"You're the boss."

This time, she came closer and put her arms around his neck, her lips finding his. This time, she opened them, and his tongue found hers and began a languid, loving dance as Harriet's body pressed against him. As her round, soft breasts pressed into his chest, his restraint disappeared, and he had to will himself not to ravish her on the spot. He felt his cock grow hard, and he let out a sigh just as Harriet's lips began to trail kisses down his neck.

"Touch me," she whispered, placing his hand on her breast.

"Your wish is my command," he said, cupping her breast, teasing the nipple to hardness as Harriet began to moan with pleasure. "Are you sure about this, sweetie?" he asked, voice gruff with desire.

"Yes," she said as her fingers found his cock.

"Oh my God!" he groaned. In the blink of an eye, clothes were flying all around until they lay naked in one another's arms.

"Condom?" she asked, looking up shyly.

"Jesus, no. Wait, wait, there's an old one in the first aid kit. Don't ask!"

He grabbed the backpack and found a small canvas bag, which he unzipped. "Eureka!" he said, holding up a foil-wrapped package. "Do you think we dare? It's probably still good."

"Who cares," she said, grabbing it and slipping it onto him, massaging him until Kyle groaned, wondering if he was going insane. Her voice and her words confirmed the insanity. He couldn't believe he heard her say, "Fuck me, Kyle Morgan, before my body explodes from wanting you."

What have you done with Harriet Winthrop? he thought as he plunged into her, lost in a crescendo of fire and passion. Their bodies moved as one as they thrust against each other, finally reaching a roaring simultaneous climax that left them spent and slick with sweat.

"Oh my goodness," she sighed, kissing his shoulder. "I do love sex!"

"You certainly do. Me too," he said, lips finding hers.

"It's been a very long time," she whispered. "And never like this."

"Good," he said, nuzzling against her. "You cold?"

"Never," she said as they drifted off to sleep.

*****

"Hey, sweetie," Kyle whispered, kissing her forehead as he tried to cover them. "While I'd like nothing better than to hold you like this all night, we're being eaten alive."

Harriet woke, wide-eyed, mosquitos buzzing all around her in the pitch dark. For a second, she wasn't sure where she was. "Oh, they're everywhere, aren't they?"

"'Fraid so. We should've kept the bracelets on when we...you know." He smiled, kissing her nose. "Sorry, I hate to do this," he said as he sat up.

Harriet groaned. "Oh, don't leave me." Then she felt along her back and legs. They were covered with bumps. "What are these?"

"Probably mostly mosquitos, but they could be chigger bites, spiders, who the hell knows till we get home in the light." Kyle rooted around in his backpack and produced a small battery-powered lantern, which he switched on so they could find their clothes scattered all around.

As Harriet dressed, she felt bites on her arms, stomach, buttocks, and up and down her neck and face. *How am I going to explain this?* she thought, smiling as she pulled on her jeans.

Kyle packed up the food and grabbed the backpack. "Thank God bears didn't find us."

"Bears?" she asked, terror in her green eyes.

"Or mountain lions. They hunt their prey and usually don't bother with leftover food."

"How reassuring," she said, tying her sneakers, then standing up and wrapping her sweater around her waist.

"Hey, I'm here to protect you." He drew her into his arms and kissing her.

"Hmm...that's a little better." Her arms circled his strong shoulders as she returned his kiss.

Reluctantly, Kyle pulled back and took her hand. "Come on. We better hightail it before there's nothing left for the bugs."

The way down was quick, and they were in the truck before she knew it. "What time is it, do you suppose?" Harriet asked as she slid into the cab.

"Just after ten fifteen. Early. Why, do you want to do something?"

Harriet laughed. "I can think of lots of things I'd like to do, but right now, I'd better get home to calamine lotion and a shower."

"How 'bout breakfast tomorrow? I have to be at work by eight thirty, but I'd love to take you to Gracie's on my way out of town."

"What time? I can meet you there," she said, already sad at the prospect of saying good night.

"Is six thirty too early?"

"Six thirty it is."

They rode back in silence, holding hands, her head resting on his strong shoulder. When Kyle pulled into Spark's, the house was mostly darkened, although the outside lights were on. "Want me to walk you in?" he asked, smiling at her.

"I'm fine. Thank you. I had fun tonight. Probably the most fun I've had in years." *If ever.*

"Me too," he said. He leaned over for a deep, lingering kiss. He reached up to cup a soft, round breast and felt his cock stand at attention. "Hey, baby," he said gruffly. "I'd better let you go, or I'll have to ravish you here on Spark's perfect lawn, bugs and all."

"Hmm…an interesting thought. It is nice and soft. Not under the floodlights, though. Night," she said and pulled away.

Her legs felt like rubber as she made her way up the walk to the house. *Tonight may have been a mistake, but at this moment, it feels just right.*

CHAPTER 17

"What happened to you two?" Gracie asked, hands on hips as she gazed down at Harriet and Kyle the next morning. "Looks like you got into poison ivy or a swarm of chiggers."

Harriet looked at Kyle and grinned. Like hers, his face was covered with tiny red dots, as were his neck and arms. "You sure have a lot of bugs out here." She smiled sheepishly at Gracie.

"Hmm… They come out after dark, but most folks apply bug repellant," Gracie said drolly.

"Give us a break, Grace, okay?"

The kind steel-gray eyes regarded him. Gracie considered Kyle and his siblings as her own kids. "What'll you two lovebirds have?"

They both ordered the omelet special, mushrooms, tomatoes, and Morgan's Run sausage.

"Is there anything you don't produce at the ranch?"

"Wine, beer, and we have some beef, but nothing like the Dillons' operation. They have the largest herd of Angus cattle in the state."

"Talk about a bread basket. All the food this valley produces is amazing," she said, suddenly noticing that he was staring. "What?"

"You do have a lot of bites. Do I look like that?" he asked, leaning back, grinning.

"Yes, you do. Maybe we shouldn't have appeared in public today."

"I'm glad we did," he said, taking her hand.

Harriet chewed on her lower lip, a habit she'd had since childhood. "Do you think we maybe jumped the gun a bit last night?"

"In what way?" he asked, knowing full well what she meant.

"I mean…we barely know each other, and suddenly, we're…you know."

He massaged her palm, sending waves of sensation through her. "Do you regret it?"

"No. Do you?"

"Not for one second. In fact, I'd take four times as many bug bites before I'd trade one minute of last night."

Harriet smiled a warm, shy smile. "Me too."

He gave her a mischievous look, his dark eyes lit up. "So, you want to do it again, tonight, no bugs?"

"To what are you referring, Mr. Morgan?"

He laughed as Maria, the waitress, set down their plates. "Dinner, of course."

"I'd love to, but I'll have to check with Mom and Spark. There was some talk of a trip into Tucson."

"Boring."

She took a bite of the delicious omelet, sighing. "Oh my goodness, Gracie's food is heaven."

"So? Tucson or…"

"I'm sure they'd be fine if I skipped out. I'll check and call later."

"I've got an idea. The camp pool is open and ready for swimming, but camp doesn't open till next week. Wanna take a swim, then have dinner in town? Or, we could dress up and go to the Red Mesa."

"I've heard about that place from Mother. Sounds lovely, and expensive. Maybe save it for a night when I don't look bedraggled after swimming?"

"I've got an idea," he said. "You find out if you're free, and I'll work on it."

"Uh-oh."

"Don't worry, it'll be bug-free. Promise."

After breakfast, they walked hand in hand to her car, one of Spark's enormous SUVs. Harriet had parked in a secluded lot behind the hardware store and walked several blocks to Gracie's. "I'm there," she said as they passed the town green.

"How 'bout you come in here," he said, gently pulling her into the woods at the edge of the green. They came to a clearing, and he leaned against a huge boulder, drawing her to him. "I wanted to kiss you without the whole town watching. Is that okay?"

She nodded, hands caressing his neck as his lips captured hers. The kiss was deep, long, and luscious as they began to move against each other, his erection tickling her tummy. "Hmm…" she murmured as he cupped both her breasts, caressing and stroking till her nipples grew hard.

"You know," he whispered. "I could lift that pretty skirt and slip you out of your panties. How would that be?"

"Done," she said, twirling her lacy pink panties on one finger.

"How did you?"

"Magic," she said, trailing kisses down his neck. "But what I want is the magic you do with this," she said, hands stroking along the buttons of his jeans, which were stretched to the max now.

"I told you last night. Your wish is my command." Like lightning, he unbuttoned himself and released his cock. "Hmm, baby, you feel so hot and wet," he said, fingers gliding in and out of her warm depths. "You ready?"

Harriet didn't trust herself to speak, but she nodded as he produced a condom and slipped it on. "Got 'em just in case," he said, grinning.

"So glad," she said, breathless with desire and longing.

Kyle grabbed hold of her round buttocks, lifted her to wrap her legs around his waist, and plunged inside her. With that first thrust, she screamed, then clapped her hand over her mouth. "Do you think anyone heard?" she whispered.

"Who cares, sweet cakes," he said as she arched her back and opened herself to him, matching his every thrust with her own.

Silently, they moved, breathing as one as they climbed to a thunderous climax. He pulled her closer as he leaned back against the smooth granite. "You're amazing."

Too spent to speak, Harriet buried her head in the crook of his shoulder and kissed his neck.

"Hey, anyone in there?" a voice called. "Everything okay?"

"Jesus," Kyle muttered, withdrawing and setting her down, smoothing her skirt.

As Harriet slipped her panties on, he zipped his jeans and straightened his T-shirt. They had barely gotten themselves together when Wilbur McGraw, owner of Valley Hardware, stepped into the clearing.

"Hey, Wilbur, mornin'," Kyle said.

"Jiminy, you kids gave me a scare. Seems like I'm always findin' one of you Morgan boys neckin' in the woods somewhere around here."

"Well, gotta get to work," Kyle said as he took Harriet's hand and led her toward the car. When they reached the SUV, they both burst into peals of laughter. "One more thing we'll have to explain. This'll be all over town by noon."

"Oh Lord," Harriet said. She was still smiling when she drove into Spark's driveway ten minutes later, the searing heat of Kyle's goodbye kiss still warm on her lips.

Harriet drove past a strange gray sedan parked in the drive and pulled the SUV around back. As she grabbed her purse, Aria stepped out the back door. "Leave the keys," she called. "I've got to head into town."

As Harriet approached, Aria's eyes grew wide. "What the hell happened to you?"

"Bug bites."

"Where were you? In the middle of a swamp?"

Harriet chuckled. "Something like that."

Aria's eyes shone with glee. "You were with him, weren't you?"

She nodded. "Despite all my talk, I plunged in after all."

Aria grinned, giving her a hug. "Good for you! Now let's find a cowboy for me, and we'll be all set. Wanta do something later? Movie or anything?"

"I'd love to, but I'm not sure how the day will unfold with my mom and all. Whose car is that in the driveway?"

"Haven't the faintest idea. I've been in the kitchen all morning. Spark's taking lunch to the crew today, and that means a mountain of sandwiches. I've gotta get drinks in town. Apparently, the guys like soda—yuck—especially Rootin' Root Beer," she said, referring to a locally produced soda brand.

Harriet waved goodbye and strolled up the back walkway. It was a beautiful day, perfect for a long hike. Selfishly, she hoped her mother's plans did not include her. She paused, looking up, closing her eyes, and felt the warmth of the sun on her face. It was the last bit of peace she would have for days.

CHAPTER 18

Helen was waiting for her in the kitchen. "Morning, Mum," Harriet said brightly. "It's beautiful out!" Then she noticed her mother's expression, grave and solemn. Not a hint of a smile. "What's wrong?"

"Sit, sweetheart. Please." Helen patted the stool beside her.

Heart in her throat, Harriet sat. "What is it? Is it Lucy or Clara or Hazel? The kids? What?"

"No, no. Everyone's fine."

As Helen spoke, Harriet noticed the fine lines now etched in her mother's lovely face. Lines that did not diminish her fragile, subtle beauty. "Then what is it? You're trembling."

"The police are here to talk to you."

"Oh?" Harriet braced herself for what was to come.

"They found him and his accomplice." Her mother still did not utter his name.

"Where? When?"

"In California, south of Los Angeles. They've been living and working in Laguna Beach."

"Why do they want to talk to me?"

"This is it, sweetheart. For almost fourteen years, we've been waiting to get justice for what he did. Now he can be punished and put in jail where he belongs."

Harriet began to shake her head. "No, no, no! I don't want it! I don't want this!"

"Harriet, please. This is what you deserve."

"No one put Dad in jail for what he did."

For a minute, her mother was struck dumb, and she sat back as if she'd been hit in the chest. Finally, she said, "This is different, and you know it."

Harriet jumped up and started pacing, banging against cabinets and counters as she reeled from side to side as if drunk. "No, no, no, I won't. I can't."

A door opened, and Spark stepped in. He took one look at Harriet and went to her side, putting his arm around her shoulders. When he spoke, his voice was firm but soothing. "Ladies, we're ready for you. We'll do this together, young lady. Be over before you know it."

Flabbergasted, Helen watched her daughter be propelled forward. Two men in suits stood in the family room. The tallest, thin with short blond hair, held a folder and came forward. "Ms. Winthrop, I'm Andy Joslin, a criminal investigator for the federal government, a US marshall." He flipped open his wallet and displayed his badge. "This is Agent Howe, FBI."

Agent Howe, with broad shoulders and curly brown hair, followed suit and showed his badge. "Good morning, ma'am."

Harriet nodded.

"Let's all sit," Spark said. "You gentlemen want something to drink?"

"No, thanks, sir," Joslin said.

Howe raised his hands, and said, "All set, thanks."

"Ladies, can I get you something?"

Helen shook her head, and Harriet stayed mute. Spark plunked Harriet on the sofa, poured a glass of water from the sideboard, and took a seat beside her. "Now then, Agent Joslin. Why don't you tell Ms. Winthrop why you're here?"

"Thank you, sir," Joslin said, opening his folder, then directing his attention to Harriet. "Our organization has arrested a con artist, Arthur Greene, and his partner, Tania Davis. I believe you knew them as Louis and Barbara Carrington?"

Joslin produced several photos and passed them to Spark, who held them in front of Harriet.

He's aged, she thought, staring at the mug shot of the man with whom she had lived on and off for almost a year. The man to whom she had given her heart and all that she had. He had a mustache and day-old beard, but it was definitely him. Barbara's hair was a different color, dark brown now instead of bleach blonde as she'd known her, but it was her. *She looks fifty*, Harriet thought, gazing up and nodding slightly to Joslin.

"They've been involved in human trafficking the past three years, and we've been watching them. Finally nabbed them and a few others last week. When we searched their apartment in Laguna, we found boxes and paperwork with your name and address. We tried to contact you through your mother and then your father. His name is on some of the paperwork. He sent us to your sister Lucy, and she sent us here. This will actually be an easier trip from Arizona to California for you."

Harriet gasped. "Excuse me?"

"We'd like you to come back with us. To identify some of your things and to testify."

Mutely, Harriet shook her head.

"This is a lot for Ms. Winthrop to take in," Spark said, his strong arm once again circling her shoulders.

"I understand that, sir, but her presence and testimony is critical. We have them dead to rights on what they've been doing out here, but what he did to Ms. Winthrop is a federal crime with a lot more mandatory prison time. We want these two locked up forever. There may even be a way for Ms. Winthrop to regain some of her assets. Forensics is scouring their bank accounts and investments now."

"No, no, no," Harriet said, standing and heading for the door.

As she hurried out, her mother on her heels, she heard Spark say, "Why don't you fellas leave your cards. Where're you stayin'?"

Helen closed the door quietly and went upstairs to find Harriet crumpled on her bed in the fetal position, sobbing. "Oh, dearie," she said, sitting beside her, patting her back.

"I know what you're going to say, Mother, but I can't. I won't! Not now, not ever!"

CHAPTER 19

"Hey, Spark, thanks, this is great," Kyle said, waving one of Aria's Northwest wraps, turkey, cheese, seasonal vegetables, and Aria's secret sauce. All the sandwiches were delicious, but the sauce made them divine. Like Carmela, Spark's chef had a few secrets up her sleeve that she would divulge to no one.

Spark smiled, never so happy than when he sat among the men and women who worked for him. "My pleasure, son."

"My turn next week," Ben Senior said. "Or, more accurately, Carmela's!"

They make work fun, Kyle thought, watching his father and his best friend. *That's something to which we can all aspire.*

"What're the ladies at your house doin' today?" Ben Senior asked. "Nora's off at Cowbelles, but I heard somethin' about us all meetin' up tonight?"

Spark's face turned solemn. His voice low, he spoke so that only his friend and Kyle could hear him. "There's been a bit of trouble this morning."

Spark went on to summarize the visit from the agents. At the end, Ben said, "Anything we can do?"

"Not at the moment, but I'll keep you posted. Harriet's in her room and won't come out. Her mom's afraid she's gonna have a breakdown."

Kyle stood, tossing his sandwich wrapper into the basket. "Dad, Spark, I've gotta take off for a while. Thanks again for lunch."

"She won't see you, son," Spark said. "Won't even talk to her mother."

Kyle waved and hurried off.

Ben shook his head, watching his son race off. "Poor baby. I can see why she wouldn't want to see the bastard. Too bad we can't give him some good ole cowboy justice. I know a few fellas who'd help with that."

*****

Kyle raced down the Gila and across town. When he arrived at the house, Aria answered the door, shaking her head. "Her mom's in the sunroom, and she's upstairs. She won't talk to anyone."

"I'd like to try. Where is she?"

Aria studied the handsome Morgan brother, whose eyes were wild. "Top of the stairs, third door on the right." As he turned away, she called, "Morgan? There's an adjoining bath off the second bedroom, where her mom's staying. You may be able to get in that way, if she won't open the door."

Kyle stared at the chef in a pristine white apron, her raven hair tied back in a ponytail. "What?"

"You heard me. Someone's gotta talk to her before she goes off the deep end. I'm guessing the best man for the job is you. She's in love with you, you know."

Kyle turned and took the stairs two at a time. *No time to think about Aria's words and whether they're true.* Spark's chef was a pot stirrer. Who knew whether to believe her? He knocked at the door and received no answer. "Harriet, it's me, Kyle," he said softly. "Please let me in."

"Not now, Kyle. Please just go away."

"Come on, just for a minute?"

"No! Go away!"

This continued for several minutes until he gave up and started for the stairs. He was just about to descend, when he paused and muttered, "What the hell," and headed back and into the other bedroom through to the enormous marble bathroom that separated mother's and daughter's rooms. Hand on the knob, he took a deep breath and slowly pushed it open.

She was on the bed, her legs drawn up practically to her chest. Her body was impossibly still. He crossed the room and sat beside her. Harriet appeared not to notice his presence until he gently touched her back. "Hey, sweetie, I'm here."

As she turned away from him, he noticed several thin scratches on her arm. As if she noticed his gaze, she covered them with her hand. "I can't right now," she said in a tiny child's voice that he would not have recognized had he not been beside her.

"I'm not leaving. Not now, not ever." He gently massaged her back.

"Please, Kyle, I can't."

In answer, he lay beside her, arm around her, head resting against the back of her neck. "It's okay, baby. It'll be okay."

He wasn't sure how long they lay there, but a knock at the door startled them. "Honey, it's me," Helen's voice called. "Can I come in?"

Kyle stood, went to the door, and opened it. Helen hugged him, whispering, "Thank you for coming."

They returned to the bedside, where Harriet still lay still and unresponsive. Helen stepped forward. "Harriet, Leonora and Maggie are downstairs."

"Mother, please!"

"They've brought someone to talk with you. She's a therapist from town. Maggie has seen her many times."

Harriet shook her head.

Helen went on. "Her name's Haley. She's coming up in five minutes. I'll leave you to collect yourself, but I am bringing her up." With that, Helen strode out the door, closing it behind her.

Instantly, Harriet sat up. "She never listens! No one listens!"

"Haley's terrific. I haven't consulted her, but my sister Beth and Maggie claim she saved their lives. Harley too, if you can believe it."

"I have a therapist," Harriet said, crossing the room to brush her hair. She looked thin in baggy sand-colored capris and a sleeveless white top. After a cursory brushing, she gazed in the mirror, then went to sit in one of the two armchairs in the window alcove. "I guess I'm having a therapy session whether I like it or not!"

"When she comes, I'll leave, but I'm staying downstairs. Okay?"

"You don't need to stay. I'm sure you have work."

"Patty can handle things. No major health crises today."

"What about Misty?"

He stood beside and took her hand. "I'm where I want to be."

Sad eyes gazed up at him. "Believe me, you should want to be a million miles away from me."

Another knock at the door and Helen stepped in with a short, round woman with long curly silver hair and deep gray eyes. "Hello, Harriet. I'm Haley," she said.

CHAPTER 20

Haley Alvarez sat in the chair opposite Harriet and nodded to the others. Kyle and Helen exited the room, closing the door behind them. "So...lovely to meet you," Haley said, settling herself in the chair. Dressed in flowing linen pants and a white linen top, she slipped out of her sandals as she leaned back and crossed her legs.

"Thank you for coming, but it really isn't necessary," Harriet said. "My mother phoned you without my permission."

"Actually, it was Leonora Morgan who called."

Harriet threw up her hands, gazing out the window at the distant mountains. "Even better!"

"Shall I go?"

Surprised by the question, Harriet turned to face her. "Honestly, I don't know. I'm in no position to make a decision about anything right now."

"Is that typical for you? I mean, do you have difficulty with decision-making in your daily life?"

"Is that what you came to talk with me about? My decision-making skills?" Harriet snapped, instantly regretting her tone.

"No, I came because your mother and your friends are concerned about you. They thought I might be able to help."

"I'm sorry, I'm being really rude. It's not your fault. I shouldn't be snapping at you."

"It's not your fault either, Harriet. From what little I know of the situation, you are the injured party here. You were a loving, generous partner who was horribly treated by someone you trusted."

"Yes, but I was also a foolish, stupid, desperate woman who let her heart run away from her."

"Oh? Why would you think that?"

"Look at the headlines. 'Heiress loses her fortune to grifters.'"

"Experienced grifters."

"Who cares?"

"While what they did, and especially what he did, was evil and despicable, grifters, the good ones, are experts at what they do. Ordinary, law-abiding people have no understanding of that kind of evil."

"You sound like you're speaking from experience."

"My first husband," Haley said softly. "But I've only told a couple of the people closest to me, and the police. No one in Saguaro is aware of my past."

"And you'd rather keep it that way?"

Haley shrugged. "It's been a long time. I don't think of it much or talk about it, but if it would help for you to tell loved ones about my admission, that would be your choice."

Harriet gave her a wan smile. "I can't imagine I'll have reason or opportunity. Did they catch him?"

"Yes."

"Did you have to testify?"

"Yes."

"Was it horrible?"

"Yes. One of the hardest days of my life."

"Would you do it again?"

"Yes."

"I'm afraid."

"Of course you are."

"Not just about seeing him again. I'm afraid I'll spiral down and lose myself in the process. Do you know that the first thing I did when I left those officers was this?" Harriet held out her arms, revealing the fresh scratches.

"It looks like you stopped yourself."

"This time. If the mention of his name brings on this, think where I'll be at the end of a day in court."

"There are ways to prepare yourself. Ways to minimize the trauma."

"Do they work?"

"Sometimes. Yes they can be quite effective."

"What are they? These ways?"

"Well, there are mind tools to strengthen your emotional state. You would also not go alone, but take a support team with you."

"I'm not sure I'm strong enough, Ms. Alvarez."

"Haley," she said, smiling. "I would guess you're more than strong enough given where you are today."

"This trip has been an emotional roller coaster."

"In what ways?"

"Out of the blue, I've begun a love affair with a man I hardly know. I panicked one day with him and am responsible for laming a horse, and now the visit from the agents or police or whoever they are this morning."

"So is the love affair a good thing, do you think?"

"Yes. I mean, I don't think he's like Arthur Greene, if that's what you're asking." Somehow, she didn't choke saying Louis's real name. *That's a start.*

"Not necessarily. I was asking if this relationship has been a positive addition to your life."

"Well, it's brand-new, but yes, it's been nice. Once I allowed myself to loosen up and let it happen."

"So you view it as something that happened *to you*?"

"Not exactly. I was a full participant. In fact, had I not acted, it wouldn't have happened. He's very considerate."

"You don't have to answer this if it's too painful," Haley said, "but would you describe the beginning of your relationship with Mr. Greene in the same way?"

"No, Arthur pursued me. Relentlessly and, in hindsight, aggressively. Flowers every morning on my doorstep, gifts, cards, poems, romantic dates to fancy, very expensive restaurants. He always paid."

"So you were wooed?"

Harriet nodded. "Yes, I guess you could say that. I was flattered, deeply. I could not believe someone could care about me like that."

"So you were in love?"

"I was in love with the idea of being loved. Arthur told me that he loved me constantly when we were together."

"So are you in love now? With this new man?"

"I don't know. It's completely different. It feels more...maybe more equal? More like friends, but there's a fierce attraction too. When he's near, when I catch sight of him, my whole body reacts. Screams for him, actually. I've never felt like that with any man. It's lovely on the one hand, but also scary."

"Do you trust him?"

Harriet hesitated, then finally said, "Yes. Yes, I do."

"Then that's a beginning, isn't it?"

"Yes, I guess it is," she said, smiling at Haley.

"That trust will make you strong, Harriet. Don't forget that."

CHAPTER 21

"You feeling better?" Kyle asked, taking her hand. They sat in a back booth at the Bulldog, which was quiet, only a half dozen patrons.

Harriet loved his touch. As his thumb gently massaged her palm, her body responded, warmth suffusing every inch of her. "Better is a relative term with me. I'm not doing myself bodily harm, so that's something," she said. "I did these scratches on my way upstairs after meeting with the agents, but by the time I got to my room, I'd talked myself down from that precipice at least. In the old days, I'd have been bleeding by the time I reached my room. Pretty ghastly, huh? I'm sure you're ready to head for the hills, and I don't blame you."

"As I told you this morning, I'm not going anywhere."

"Why? What could possibly make you want to hang around with me?"

He smiled. "Is that what we're doing? Hanging around?"

She blushed, returning his smile. "Well, maybe a little bit more than hanging."

"You look pretty tonight," he said.

And she did in a pale green linen sundress, its neckline revealing a hint of cleavage. She always felt a bit wanton in this particular dress, but it was cool and she'd thrown it into her suitcase at the last minute. Now she was glad she had.

"Thank you. You too, but you Morgan men would look gorgeous in burlap sacks."

"I doubt that. Kinda itchy, don't you think?"

Russ Keeler appeared, pad in hand. "Hey, folks, what can I get you?"

Kyle ordered a Bulldog Burger and Harriet a grilled chicken salad. They each ordered a Desert Amber, and Russ disappeared, with "Sure enough."

"I'm not a big beer drinker, but I like your local brew," she said.

"Yeah, it's pretty good, though I'll take your Sam Adams or a Newcastle any day."

"Do you miss Boston?"

"Sometimes, but as I've told you before, this is home."

"You must be really excited about the farm. Are the horses all healthy?"

"So far, so good. And before you ask, Misty's much improved. I think she's gonna be fine, and Ned agrees. We rigged up a sling, and she's been okay with it. Some horses go nuts, but Misty's a calm, sweet girl. Takes everything in her stride."

"If all hell hadn't broken loose today, I had planned to go down and visit her. Would it be okay if I went tomorrow?"

"What's happened with California?"

Her face clouded over as she spoke. "I told them I'd give them my answer in the morning."

Kyle took her hands in his, gazing into her gentle, sad eyes. "Do you know what that answer will be?"

"I'll go. The arraignment is the day after tomorrow in Santa Ana. Agent Joslin says that's the only time they'll need me. To…to identify him and then to go to Laguna to look over the materials in their apartment. I can't guarantee that I'll keep it. Sanity, I mean."

"You'll do fine."

Tears sprang to her eyes. "You don't know him," she said as Russ set down their beers and retreated without a word.

Kyle gripped her hands. "I know he's a bastard who deserves to be locked up for the rest of his life."

Harriet shook her head from side to side. "I loved him. I mean…not the way I feel about you, but I was infatuated. Gaga, blind, and stupid."

"I'm coming with you."

"What?"

"I'm coming to California with you."

"Absolutely not. You're just starting a new job. Mother will come with me."

"I've already spoken to your mom, and she agrees. Spark's plane is ready to take us, and he'll have a car waiting at the airport. We can stay with Buck or at a hotel. Your choice."

As Harriet stared at this kind, gentle man whom she had met less than a week ago and who was willing to put his life on hold for her, tears rolled down her cheeks. "Oh, Kyle, I don't know what to say."

Kyle gazed up and winked at Russ as the tavern owner set down their food. "Thanks, buddy."

"My pleasure. Wave if you need anything," Russ said as he left them alone.

"There's nothing to say, sweetheart. You need a friend, and I'm it. So that's that. This food looks great, doesn't it?"

Harriet barely ate a bite as he devoured his burger. Several times, Kyle offered her some of his food, in case her salad was "off," but she declined, sipping her beer, picking at the salad. As they walked to his truck arm in arm, she asked, "Would be too much for us to pop by the stables and peek in at Misty?"

"You read my mind," he said, squeezing her shoulder as he drew her closer.

CHAPTER 22

The barn was shrouded in darkness as Kyle parked the truck. "Everyone's gone for the night," he said as he took her hand. Just inside the door, he flipped a switch, and the space was illuminated with soft light from six hanging bulbs at various spots along the length of the barn. The soft nickering and snuffing of the horses followed them until they reached Misty's stall and Kyle switched on the single bulb hanging from the rafters.

"Oh my goodness," Harriet said softly, spying the enormous white horse dangling a half inch from the floor. A canvas sling was wrapped round her belly.

"She can put her hooves down, but they don't carry weight."

"I've never seen anything like it," Harriet said from the doorway. "Will it unsettle her if I pet her?"

In answer, he stepped into the stall and petted Misty's muzzle. "Hey, big girl," he said softly. "You've got a visitor."

Tentatively, Harriet came forward and touched her soft nose. "Hi, sweetie. What a brave girl you are." Misty nickered, throwing her head up, and Harriet stepped behind him.

"Don't be startled. That's her way of saying hello," he said, rubbing the horse's nose.

They petted Misty for several more minutes, then stepped out of the stall and turned off the light. "Night, sweet girl," Harriet said softly.

Kyle led her past the stalls to the back corrals, then sat and patted the bench beside him. "This is one of my favorite spots on the ranch," he said.

"What makes it special?"

"Well, I like the view, but mostly I like the possibilities that dance around you when you sit here."

"Very poetic," she said softly. "Please tell me more."

"At any one time, there could be three or four lessons goin' on, a trainer could be working with a horse, pack trips could be starting off or returning. It's the hub of the ranch. It's where I learned to ride and love horses. This is where I found my life's work. People I care about work here. It's a great crew."

Harriet nodded. "I don't think I've met anyone here that wasn't wonderful."

He grinned. "What about your new best friend?"

In the darkness, she couldn't read his expression. "Who do you mean? Oh, you mean Aria?"

"Ignore me. I'm an asshole."

"She's actually really nice and fun. I spend more time in the kitchen with her than with Mother and Spark."

"An acquired taste," he said.

"What do you have against her anyway?"

"When she first arrived she came on like gangbusters, chasing every guy within twenty miles."

"I haven't noticed that," Harriet said, gazing out into the night. "I think she's a bit lonely."

"Yeah? Maybe that's been it all along. She chased poor Nick around for weeks, but that's finally cooled down."

"He wasn't interested?" she asked.

"Nick's gay. He doesn't advertise it, and I don't think he's with anyone at the moment."

"Mother says he's an amazing trainer. A horse whisperer?"

"He's pretty incredible. No one relates to horses like he does, which is why Harley's been tryin' to poach him for the thoroughbred farm."

"Will he go?"

"That depends. My dad would have to okay it. I'm pretty certain if Nick asked to go, he wouldn't stand in his way. It would be a big promotion for him, and he could still consult down here. Poor Maggie has already lost Harley, then Jeb to school, now maybe Nick. They're actively looking for at least one full-time person here, maybe two."

As he spoke, Kyle twirled a lock of her hair around his finger. "You are an extraordinary woman, babe."

She gazed over at him, her fingers reaching up to trace the line of his strong jaw. "Ordinarily, I dislike that word 'babe,' but when you say it, it sounds really sexy."

"Which you are. Really sexy, I mean."

He leaned over, his lips capturing hers. Harriet responded, her tongue finding his as her body responded. Suddenly, she pulled back. "Do you think this is appropriate given what we'll be doing tomorrow?"

"Not only appropriate, but essential. Come here," he said gruffly, pulling her onto his lap. "You are so beautiful, babe."

As his lips trailed hot kisses down her neck, Harriet cried out. "Oh, Kyle, that feels…that feels…oh, oh, oh!"

As he nibbled her breasts through the thin fabric of her dress, his hand reached under her skirt, sliding her panties aside. She was wet and so ready for him. "Say when, babe."

In answer, Helen stood and stepped away from his magic fingers that were already threatening to take her over the edge. She smiled at him as she slipped her panties off and straddled him. With deft fingers, she unbuttoned his jeans. "Condom, please?" She could sense more than actually see his wide grin as he slipped a condom from his back pocket. "You came prepared, Mr. Morgan."

"Always, just in case," he said, then groaned as she slipped the condom onto him, stroking and caressing. "Jesus Christ!" he said as he drew her closer. "You ready, babe?"

"Mmm," she murmured, moving closer until his cock tickled her. "So, so, ready, cowboy."

As he plunged into her moist depths, drawing her closer, Harriet cried out. He had touched a place so deep inside her that, for an instant, she felt torn apart. Then her body opened, and she arched her back, taking him deeper. In the darkness, their bodies moved as one, the only sounds their breathing and the creak of the old bench.

"Take me, take me, take me," Harriet cried as her body writhed in a blinding explosion of sensation.

"Oh babe, I'm tryin', I'm tryin'."

As they climaxed, Harriet almost stood above him, then collapsed in his arms, spent and sated beyond anything she had ever experienced. The angst and pain of the day and the horror of the ordeal ahead fell away as she settled into his loving embrace. Her legs shook as she nestled her head in the crook of his shoulder. "I can do it," she whispered, kissing his neck.

"Hmm?"

"I can do the court thing. All I'll have to do is think back to this, and Arthur Greene will be no more than a gnat to me."

"That's the spirit, babe," he said, kissing her softly. "And I'll wink and gesture from the gallery in case I think you've forgotten."

When Harriet stepped into Spark's front hall, every inch of her body felt warm and peaceful. Helen spied her and saw the change. *Thank you, Kyle Morgan*, she thought to herself as she came out of the study to greet her daughter.

CHAPTER 23

The next day was a blur of activity—packing, phone calls, and arrangements were made for the trip west. In the end, the party included Helen, Harriet, Spark, Aria, and Kyle. Leonora had offered to come along, but Helen thanked her, saying they'd be fine. The elder Morgans brought a basket of food and their son to the Grenville Airport.

"Good luck, darlin'," Ben Senior said, his kind blue eyes gazing down at her.

Harriet gave him and Leonora hugs.

"Thank you. I'm so grateful to you both."

"Hey, Mom, Dad," Kyle said, hugging them as he joined the others.

"Call us, honey. When it's over," Leonora whispered.

"Will do."

As the party disappeared into the plane, Leonora turned to her husband. "I hope he knows what he's getting into."

"We raised him right, darlin'. If they're meant to be together, he'll take care of her and she him. Just like you and me."

"I know, I just worry. That's all."

"That's one of the many things I love about you," he said, kissing the top of her head. They waved as the plane taxied down the runway.

*****

The flight to John Wayne Airport in Santa Ana was quick and they landed before anyone had thought to touch the basket of food. "We'll bring it along to Buck's," Spark said. "He never has any food in the condo."

Buck greeted them on the tarmac and grabbed their bags. His condo had three bedrooms, and he had arranged for the ladies to stay in a nearby unit whose owner, a good friend, was out of town.

"Let's get you settled. I have dinner reservations at eight. Carmela's food can be lunch or dinner tomorrow."

"If it's all the same to you," Harriet said, "I'd rather stay in. I can nibble on whatever the Morgans sent."

"Then we'll all stay in," Buck said. "I can order food if needed."

"Absolutely not," Harriet said. "I insist you all go. Have a nice dinner. I want to collect my thoughts before tomorrow."

"Well, I can stay," Helen said.

"Or me?" Aria said.

"No, please. All of you, go and enjoy yourselves."

After they unpacked, the group had a cocktail together, then prepared to go.

"I'm fine, Mother, really," she said as she hugged Helen and Aria. "Enjoy!"

"Are you sure?" Aria asked, hands on hips. She was dressed in skintight white capris and a diaphanous purple top, its neckline plunging to reveal her ample cleavage and pure white skin. It was a flattering outfit, accented with silver lamé flip-flops and large silver hoop earrings.

"Very sure," Harriet said, smiling at her. "Aria?" she asked as her friend turned back. "Thank you so much for coming."

"My pleasure." Aria squeezed her hand. "You're gonna do great."

The door closed behind the others, and Harriet closed her eyes. While she wasn't sorry to have a break from her dear mother's hovering, she felt lonely in the strange, albeit luxurious, condominium. She thought back to Kyle's arms around her the previous evening and realized that she had never felt completely warm until she met him. All those childhood years shivering in the cold dank closet among the coats that smelled of pipe tobacco, moth balls, and cologne. Even when her mother joined her, holding her tight, the cold remained like a ribbon of ice around her heart.

As she began to shake, the door opened and Kyle walked in. Oblivious to his presence, Harriet curled into herself, imagining she could hear her father's drunken curses as he pursued her mother from room to room. Finally, the dull sound of hitting would reach the closet, and Harriet would begin the relentless scratching and tearing of flesh until red stains appeared on her sleeves and nightgown.

"Hey, babe, "I'm here," Kyle said, kneeling in front of her chair, pulling her onto his lap, cradling her, rocking until she opened her eyes and came back to him.

Her immediate reaction was to peer down at her arms, looking for fresh wounds. The sigh of relief when she saw only pale, smooth skin was deep and mournful. She rested her head on his shoulder, unable to speak. Kyle held her for a long while until he sensed her body settle and respond.

Harriet sat up and gazed into his beautiful dark eyes. "Ghosts. I guess I had a spell. I get those sometimes if I let myself go back. All this, the court and all, must churn it up."

"Trauma is trauma."

"It's not that I haven't tried to let go," she said, moving away to sit beside him. "Years of therapy with a terrific person have helped me function in society, but I'm very careful. I don't see my father, except on rare occasions when I'm there to support my mom."

"That must be rough for both of you."

She shrugged. "Mum's tough, and he's not like he was. He's broken and sick. He looks like her grandfather. Still loves her despite a second wife and a string of girlfriends a mile long. They're all after his money, of course."

She looked over at him as he listened quietly, his hand on her knee. "Listen to me, going on and on when you come from such a normal, stable family."

"I'm lucky."

"Mum says that Dad wasn't always like the man I knew growing up. She says he was kind and loving and warm when they met. It was his family and going back to New Bedford that changed him. Gran was a nightmare. The nastiest person I've ever met. She hated Mum because her precious son loved his beautiful young wife more than her."

"Did you know your grandparents then?"

"Not for too long. They died when I was l little, but we lived with them, you see. Then we stayed in that horror of a house after they died. Until Mum finally escaped. She would have gone much sooner, but she was afraid she'd lose us. The Winthrop money would have seen to that."

"What about her parents, her family?"

"Her parents died when she was a baby, and she was raised by two maiden aunts, but Hildy and Adelaide died many years ago, around the time she married my father. Beyond the aunts, she had no one."

"So she escaped to your Horseshoe Crab Cove?"

Harriet smiled. In the growing twilight, even with blotchy, tear-stained cheeks, she looked beautiful. "Yes, she did. Soon after she arrived, she and her newfound friends started the Darn Yarners, and that was it. She had found her home and a new family. Thank God."

She took his hand, and they sat in silence for several minutes. Finally, she said, "You hungry?"

"Starved."

Harriet stood up. "I've got an idea to break the gloom. One of the first things my therapist taught me was the importance of breaking the gloom. Have a good cry, pick myself up, and find ways to break the gloom. So...what do you say we find a backpack, grab some of this food, and have a beach picnic? I saw bug spray in the bathroom. If you grab that, I'll see if I can find a beach towel or two."

"Will do," he said, hopping up and disappearing.

When he returned, Harriet had opened the basket and laid out enough food for twenty people. The basket was lined with cold packs, so everything was fresh and cool. They each selected sandwiches, chips, and bottles of water and packed them in a backpack she'd found in the front hall closet. Kyle opened the fridge and loaded in the remaining food.

"Hey, there's a nice bottle of white wine in here and tons of beer. We can replace them tomorrow. What do you say?"

"I say take whatever you want, but I think I'll stick with water tonight. I want to be clearheaded in the morning. Tomorrow night? As my mom's friend Frankie says, 'Katie, bar the door.' I'll drink whatever's put in front of me."

Kyle closed the fridge. "Water's good for me. Let's go."

The condo hung over the beach, which was accessible by a long, steep staircase at the south side of the building. Once her feet hit the sand, still warm from the day's heat, Harriet paused and took a deep breath. "I love the beach," she said. "One of my favorite places at home. And this will be my first time on a Pacific beach."

"Not quite like your huge expanses of sand, right?"

"It depends."

"When my brother Ben lived in Santa Barbara, we came out a few times. Beaches are much wider. This is a Laguna-style beach—craggy cliffs, riptide, and beautiful sunsets."

A few groups dotted the beach as they walked south for five minutes, wading in the calm surf as they proceeded. Finally, they rounded an outcropping of rocks and boulders and found themselves on a secluded stretch with no one in sight. "What do you think?" Kyle asked.

"Perfect. Unless the tide's coming in and we get stranded." Harriet pointed to the outcropping, which was surely underwater at high tide.

"I think we're safe for a while. We can monitor what's happening," he said, spreading the two towels and setting the backpack on one.

They sat side by side, shoulders touching as he unpacked the food. "This is nice," she said a few minutes later as they nibbled Carmela's delicious portabella baguettes.

"Sure is." He took her hand and brought it to his lips.

"Kyle, thank you for staying back tonight."

"Nowhere else I'd rather be."

She rested her head on his shoulder. They gazed out at the ocean and the fiery hues of the setting sun. Later, sandwich wrappers stowed, they lay back and watched the stars come out.

"I could stay here forever," she said, taking his hand, her fingers stroking his palm.

"Me too."

"You know what would make this even more perfect?" Harriet asked, gazing over, a mischievous look in her eye.

"Tell me, please," he said, grinning.

"If you made love to me."

"Are you sure?"

"Yes," she said softly turning on her side and beginning to stroke his erection, clearly visible in the moonlight.

He lay still. Her touch was driving him crazy, but he wanted her to be in control. Finally, he turned to face her. "You know I won't be able to hold on much longer, don't you?"

In answer, she rose, unzipped his shorts, and released him, bending to take him into her mouth, her lips and tongue everywhere. Kyle moaned as she worked her magic, and he finally let go.

"Oh my God, babe. That was incredible."

She knelt above him, smiling. "Good. I'm glad."

"But what about you wanting me to make love to you?" he asked, pulling her down for a kiss.

"The night is young," she said, responding to his kiss, straddling him.

"Yes, it is." He sat up and gently laid her on the towel. "My turn."

Harriet wore capris and a light T-shirt, which were discarded in a flash to reveal her glorious breasts in a lacy white bra and matching panties. She shimmered in the moonlight as he bent to unhook the clasp of her bra, his mouth taking one, then the other breast, nibbling, sucking and teasing until Harriet writhed with pleasure.

With one fluid motion, the panties slipped off, and his tongue and lips began a slow, delicious journey from breasts down her tummy. As he kissed and licked her, his fingers slipped between her legs, finding her wet and warm. Soon his lips and tongue replaced fingers as he buried his face between her legs, reveling in the taste of her. Harriet arched her hips, rising to meet him. Delirious, she cried out, "Kyle, Kyle, Kyle," as glorious waves of orgasm washed over her.

As she settled, he captured her lips. She could taste herself, a sensation that roused every inch of her, and she rubbed against him, reaching down to stroke his cock, already hard. "Wow, you're amazing, Kyle Morgan."

"If it's okay, I've got a condom right here," he said, grabbing his shorts.

"Okay?" Harriet smiled up at him. "My body is literally screaming for you. I want you. Deep, deep, deep inside me. Please!"

"That's my girl," he said.

Kyle lifted her legs, wrapping them around him as he slipped into the glorious warmth. Harriet met him thrust for thrust as they moved together. Before she knew what was happening, he had turned them over, and she now straddled him, her breasts accessible to his hungry lips. She arched her back, riding him, loving every sensation as they rose to a blinding explosive climax. Afterward, he pulled her close, his cock still inside her. "Oh, babe," he said as he kissed her neck and pulled one of the towels over her, their bodies cradled by the warm sand.

"Thank you for tonight," Harriet whispered.

"My pleasure sweetie."

Some time later, they lay still entwined when cold startled them. "Oh, Kyle, look," she cried, moving to her side, groaning as they separated. "We fell asleep. The tide!"

Both hopped up and grabbed their clothes, some already damp from the surf. They rescued the backpack just as it threatened to wash out to sea. Towels soaked now, they were covered with sand. Laughing, they dressed quickly and headed toward the outcropping where the surf now crashed against the boulders.

"It's okay," he said, grabbing her hand. "It's pretty shallow still. Come on!"

Soaked through by the time they reached the condo steps, they found their sandals and hurried up. When they reached the condo, he turned and gave her a deep, lingering kiss. When they broke apart, he said, "I'm guessing your mom's on the other side of this door. Are you ready?"

Laughing, she nodded. "As the song goes, 'Let's give 'em something to talk about.'"

CHAPTER 24

Harriet's head pounded when she opened her eyes. She smiled as she recalled the scene the previous evening when she opened the condo door to find Helen and Aria waiting. They knew she'd been with Kyle as he had begged out of dinner, but the look on their faces when they spied her wet and bedraggled had been priceless. Before either could speak, she had raised her hands, stating, "I'm fine. We had a beach picnic, and the tide came in. I'm covered with sand. I'm going to shower, and I'll see you in the morning."

It was six fifteen, and they were due in court at eight thirty. Buck advised that they leave by seven thirty, so she barely had time for yoga and a shower to clear her head. When she emerged, dressed in a beige pencil skirt, sleeveless white blouse, and pale cotton cardigan, she felt marginally better. Aspirin helped the head, but her body trembled with a chill that belied the warmth of the morning. Aria had set out breakfast things and made a frittata and scones. She and Helen sat at the glass-topped dining table chatting as Harriet came in.

"Morning, dearie," Helen said brightly. Dressed in a gray linen suit Harriet last remembered seeing at a funeral, her mother looked lovely, albeit understated, which was appropriate given the occasion. "As you can see, Aria has provided us with a banquet here. Come have something."

The chef eyed her. "Mornin'!" she said. "I'm gonna leave you two ladies and get changed. Be out in ten."

Helen poured her a cup of coffee and passed cream and sugar across the table. "Frittata? It's excellent. The fruit's lovely too, and oh my goodness, these scones!"

"I'm fine, Mum. Just a little cold."

"Oh dear, did you catch cold last night?"

"No, it's a thinking kind of cold. I'll be fine once this is over."

"Of course you will."

Harriet reached for a scone, which she nibbled at along with a few blueberries. "Where'd all this food come from?"

"Spark gave Buck a list. He stocked the fridges before we arrived, very liberally, I believe. All the liquor is his as well as the groceries."

She gave her mother a tired smile. "They don't make many men like Spark."

"No, they don't. He's worked hard, is very successful, and has learned the art of living well. He's also very generous and wants to share his good fortune and way of living with those he cares about."

"And we are the lucky recipients," she said, jumping as they heard the doorbell.

"It's open," Helen called.

Spark, Buck, and Kyle stepped in, all three in impeccable dark suits, Buck's offset with a pale green shirt and floral tie, Spark in a blue dress shirt and a conservative patterned tie, and Kyle also in blue dress shirt, a striped tie of navy and red knotted loosely round his neck. *Three gorgeous men,* Harriet thought as Aria whistled.

"Ladies, if we aren't the bees knees today with these guys." Aria looked lovely in a simple white sheath, a pink sweater draped over one shoulder, and strappy five-inch heels that showcased her beautiful long legs.

Kyle grinned, looking at Harriet. "We're goin' for the Good Fellas look, or maybe California posse? 'Don't mess with our gals.' Does it work?"

Helen smiled. "Yes, I believe it does. Have you all eaten?"

"What d'ya think we're doing here?" Buck asked. "I don't do breakfast."

The frittata, fruit, and every crumb of scone disappeared in short order. Kyle sat beside Harriet and took her hand under the table. He never let go until Spark announced that it was time to go. This meant that he needed to eat with his left hand as Harriet leaned against him, soaking in the warmth.

The ride to the courthouse in Santa Ana was quiet. They cruised along the highway in Spark's stretch limo, making good time. The driver pulled up at the Ronald Reagan Federal Building and US Courthouse at eight ten. Just inside security, they met Spark's Portland attorney, Fred Butler, who was licensed to practice in federal court as well as in California. He had assured them that Harriet didn't need an attorney for her testimony, but he was happy to fly down to accompany them.

Short and wiry, Spark's attorney bore an uncanny resemblance to Woody Allen except for his dark, curly hair and intense dark eyes. Having worked in a high-end men's shop during college, Harriet knew men's suits, and Butler's suit cost at least three thousand dollars, maybe more.

Fred came forward and shook everyone's hands. "I've found a room for us upstairs. Follow me."

They entered what appeared to be a break room with coffeepot and other things on a table in the corner and a number of chairs and small tables scattered about. Fred sat at one and gestured for them to join him. There were four seats. Harriet took one, Kyle beside her, their hands still clasped, and Spark sat beside Fred. Helen, Aria, and Buck sat to the side.

Fred smiled at Harriet. "I see you've brought your support team."

"Yes."

Butler reached across the table and patted her free hand. "Ms. Winthrop, we're going to get you in and out of here as quickly as possible. Then we'll head down to Laguna Beach to identify any of your belongings still in Greene's possession. You won't be able to take them now, but I will assure that they are returned as soon as possible. Does that sound okay?"

Harriet nodded, the lump in her throat rendering her speechless.

"I'm sure this is the last place you would choose to be on a beautiful California day, but your testimony will add weight to the evidence the feds already have, ensuring that Mr. Greene and his accomplice will never hurt another person in this lifetime."

"If they have so much, why do they need me?"

"They're establishing a pattern of many years' duration. Apparently, there were a number of other women preyed upon by these two before and after your experience."

"Are they? Will they?"

"Some have disappeared, but the ones they located refused to testify. So, you see, your brave decision is very important to them."

Harriet's eyes widened, and she began to tremble. "But why wouldn't they come forward? Are they afraid he'll harm them? Am I putting myself and my family in danger?"

"No, nothing like that, my dear. For the most part, the women Agent Joslin located are on the East Coast and could not get away on such short notice. It was their luck that you were nearby."

"But trials are delayed all the time. Why not give the others time to get here?"

"Harriet," he said, holding her with his bright, arresting gaze. "It's going to be fine. I may have misspoken. They may well bring some of the others. Agents of the federal government can be very closemouthed about their plans when conversing with us civilians. What they need you to do is answer their questions truthfully and be on your way. Can you do that?"

Harriet nodded as a tear snaked down her cheek. Kyle sat beside her, inwardly cursing the lawyer for alarming her, yet knowing this was nothing compared to the ordeal ahead.

"Okay, then," Butler said. "You folks can go in and take a seat at the back of the courtroom. Ms. Winthrop and I will remain on the bench in the hall until she's called."

Everyone rose to go except Kyle. He looked up at Butler. "Can I stay with her?"

"Of course, but the courtroom will be closed when we're called, so if you stay, you'll need to remain outside while Harriet testifies."

"No!" she said. "I want him there."

Butler nodded. "Then off you go, Mr. Morgan."

Kyle turned to her, taking her hands. "I'll be there the whole time, babe. Just think of last night and say what you have to say. Okay?"

Harriet nodded, her face a mask of desperation and fear.

Kyle kissed her cheek. As he rose, he whispered, "I love you," before disappearing with the others.

"Those Morgan boys are charmers, aren't they?" Fred said. "Come on, let's get this over with so we can cruise down to Laguna in Spark's fancy limo."

In spite of herself, Harriet laughed as she stood and followed Fred Butler into the hallway.

CHAPTER 25

"Please state your whole name."

"Harriet Adelaide Winthrop."

"Ms. Winthrop, do you swear to tell the truth, the whole truth, and nothing but the truth, so help you God?"

"I do."

"You may be seated."

The man she faced now was a stranger, with short, wavy blond hair, bright blue eyes, a gray suit, and the shiniest shoes she'd ever seen. "I'm Jonathan Parrish, assistant US Attorney. I'm the prosecutor in this case. The government thanks you for coming today."

Harriet stared at Parrish's blue eyes as if they were the depths of the ocean. If she dove in, she would be safe and wouldn't have to look across the courtroom at Louis. She knew Kyle was in the back row, to the far right. When entering the room and making her way to the witness box, she had taken care to look straight ahead. With any luck, she would only be asked to glance at the defendant once, according to Butler.

"Now, then. We have you here today to testify in the case against Arthur Greene, whom you knew as Louis Carrington. Is that correct?"

She nodded, still focused on the attorney's eyes. "Yes."

"Do you see Mr. Greene aka Mr. Carrington in this court?"

Harriet froze, unable to take her eyes from the prosecutor. A quick glance at his witness and Parrish stepped back with a flourish, giving Harriet a direct line of vision to the defendant. Louis sat smug and impassive. As their eyes met, he smirked. That did it. *After all the years and all he's taken from me—my dignity and possessions—Louis Carrington, Arthur Greene, or whoever he is has no right to smirk at me!* Harriet took a deep breath and said, "Yes, he's sitting right there. Older and less dashing, perhaps, but that's him." The look on Louis's face emboldened her as she gazed out and found Kyle before returning her attention to Parrish.

"What was the nature of your relationship with Mr. Greene?"

"He was my boyfriend for over a year. We were planning to marry but were not yet formally engaged."

"Did you live together?"

"Not officially, but he spent many nights at my home."

"And you at his?"

"Rarely."

"And why was that?"

"Excuse me?"

"Why did you not spend more time at Mr. Greene's dwelling?"

"Well, for one thing, my apartment was closer to work and school. He only had a room in a boarding house-type place. It was furnished, but maybe not as comfortable."

"Did the difference in your living quarters alarm you?"

"Not really. A number of my friends lived in similar places." Harriet sensed movement from the left side of the room and saw Louis leaning over, whispering to his attorney.

"But Mr. Greene wasn't a student, was he?"

"No, he was a financial advisor."

"Didn't you find it odd with that kind of job that he would live in such squalor?"

"The apartment was neat. Just small and sparsely furnished. Louis told me he was indifferent to his home surroundings as he practically lived at the office. He also said he was saving and waiting until he could build his dream home. Our dream home."

"Is it accurate to say that you were in a committed relationship?"

"Yes."

"Please tell the court what happened? What changed?"

"The spring of graduation, we began planning the future. He gave up his room and was mostly with me, but was away several nights a week, supposedly on business trips."

"Supposedly?"

"I began to grow alarmed at his behavior. It was increasingly erratic, and he was frequently irritable and out of sorts. I should go back a bit to say that we opened a joint bank account in March of that year. He said it would be easier that way as we both got jobs and began contributing to the account."

"Did Mr. Greene bring any assets to this account?"

"Yes. When we opened the account, he put fifteen thousand dollars in."

"And you?"

"The same. I also transferred the oversight of my family trust to his firm. I looked into it beforehand. What I didn't know was that he, Mr. Greene, had been a temp on the cleaning staff for a few days and had nothing to do with the firm. He handled the transfer."

"And then?" Parrish stepped closer and blocked her view of the defendant.

"As I said, his behavior was becoming stranger and stranger. One day while I was home, I mentioned it to my sister and brother-in-law, and before I knew it, Will, my brother-in-law, had hired a private investigator. The investigator, Frankie Brown soon discovered that Mr. Greene had no association with the investment firm beyond the few days he'd spent as janitor. Frankie also learned that the woman with whom Louis was working was not his sister but a fellow con artist. Sadly, by the time we heard from Frankie it was too late. When I returned home that night, he and his partner had vanished and with them my money as well as anything of value in my apartment."

"Again, Ms. Winthrop, is the man responsible for these terrible things in this courtroom?"

"Yes, he's sitting right there." Harriet pointed to Louis.

As Parrish said, "Let the record show that the witness has identified the defendant." Harriet's eyes found Kyle, and he smiled, mouthing the words, *Great job. I love you.*

"If it please the court," Parrish added, "I have no more questions for this witness."

The judge gazed at the defendant's table. "Does the defense have questions of this witness?"

A tall blonde in a red suit and stiletto heels rose, straightening the plunging neckline of her cream-colored silk blouse. "Yes, Your Honor, I do."

CHAPTER 26

"Now, Ms. Winthrop, "I'm Calla Ross, Mr. Greene's attorney. Let's go back to your time with Arthur," defense attorney said, leaning into the witness box so closely, Harriet could smell a hint of garlic on her breath and her strong, cloying perfume. "You were in love with Mr. Greene, were you not?"

"I thought I was." Even though the woman repulsed her, Harriet couldn't quite pull her emotions together. She began to tremble. As she began to melt down, she wondered who was paying Calla Ross's fee. Her jewelry alone would have bought Harriet's house twice over.

"People do impetuous things when they're in love, don't they?"

Harriet caught Kyle's eye, and his warm smile pulled her back from the abyss. "I've never been described as impetuous, Ms. Ross."

"Maybe not, but love changes us."

Parrish rose from his seat. "Objection! Your Honor, does Ms. Ross have a question? Also, I respectfully request that she step back from the witness box."

"Objection sustained," the judge said, gazing down at Ross. "Step back, Ms. Ross, and get to the point. Now."

"Of course, Your Honor," she said, bowing slightly. "So, Ms. Winthrop, you were in love. Maybe a tad more attached to my client than he was you? You wanted to do something for him and you—"

"Objection!" Parrish cried. "Now Ms. Ross is testifying!"

The judge narrowed his brows, clearly losing patience. "Ms. Ross, get to the point or sit down."

As the exchange went on, something snapped in Harriet, and she sat up straighter. Ross saw it and circled warily. For a second, she wondered if the woman was going to sit down, but then Ross turned, eying her sharply. "You were in love with Mr. Greene. You wanted to give him something. You did, and then things didn't go your way, so you reported him to the police. What man would want to stay in that kind of relationship?"

"Objection! Parrish cried, his face beet red.

"Ms. Ross, you are now in contempt," the judge said. "I suggest that you sit or find some other line of questioning."

Ross threw up her hands, shrugged to the jury, and strolled toward the defense table. "Nothing further for this *witness*," she said, her voice dripping with sarcasm.

Parrish, who was still standing, said, "Your Honor, may I redirect?"

"Yes, go ahead."

"Harriet, Ms. Ross has painted a picture. Do you find it accurate?"

Surprised by the question, Harriet stared at him, then gazed over at Kyle.

"Objection!" Calla Ross said, hopping up.

"To what?" the judge asked.

"To making assumptions about my questioning of this witness."

"Sit down, Ms. Ross. Mr. Parrish, proceed. Ms. Winthrop, you may answer the question."

"No, it wasn't accurate. Mr. Greene led me to believe he was as in love with me as I was him. As soon as he had access to my accounts, some of which I did not give him, and he discovered through hacking, he took all of my inheritance, ransacked my home, and disappeared."

"And did you ever hear from him again?"

"Never."

"Thank you, Ms. Winthrop. One more question. At the moment, Mr. Greene and his accomplice are also accused of human trafficking, children specifically. Did you ever suspect him of such activities when you knew him?"

"Objection!" Ross said.

"I'll allow it," the judge said.

"No, nothing like that," Harriet said softly.

"Thank you, Ms. Winthrop. You are free to go. My officers will escort you to the defendant's condo so that you can identify belongings that may be yours."

"Objection! The contents of Mr. Greene's dwelling are lawfully his. There is no way to prove otherwise."

"I'm afraid you're wrong about that," Parrish said, not waiting for the judge to rule. "We have police reports from almost a dozen victims listing missing things, many of which were catalogued and photographed prior to their disappearance."

"Overruled," the judge said as Harriet stood and walked toward the door.

As she passed the defendant's table, Louis winked. Instead of cowering, she smiled back, a smile of triumph that wiped the smirk off her former lover's face. *He looks about sixty*, she mused as she made her way to the door and into the arms of her loved ones. *And I'm free of him forever. Louis Carrington can't hurt me anymore.*

CHAPTER 27

The Greenes' apartment was on a side street in the beachfront community several blocks from the ocean and considerably humbler than Buck's condominium complex. The building looked like a cheap motel, its neon-green trim faded and hanging off in several spots. The Greenes' unit was on the second floor behind a rickety green wrought iron gingerbread-style railing. Yellow police tape crisscrossed the front door. Joslin nodded at the officer on watch, who pulled the tape aside, and they entered. Mildew and neglect greeted them as they adjusted their eyes from the glare of the sun to the dark interior. "Yuck," Aria said.

"Ms. Firorelli, we will need you and the others to wait outside, please."

Helen, Kyle, Spark, Buck, and Aria waited while Harriet wandered through the space, wishing she was a million miles away. Open boxes were everywhere, and jewelry was laid out on a table. She recognized several pieces. One of the officers separated these and took photos. A small painting by John Singer Sargent stood against a wall in the closet. It had belonged to her grandparents and was one of the few things she had inherited from Hill House. She had meant to donate it to the Fine Arts Museum and intended to do so once it came back to her.

"We found a number of documents we think might be yours. These are in evidence. We also found a file stuffed with bonds for a mill in New Bedford."

"Those are worthless," Harriet said, remembering Louis's keen interest in them years ago. "Not sure why he bothered to take them. Maybe in his haste, he just scooped them up."

She was surprised to find some of her clothes in one of the closets. "You can donate all that," she said, waving.

"That's about it," Mrs. Winthrop," Joslin said. "If anything else turns up, we'll be in touch. The Greenes may have a storage unit. We're still checking. We also have the photos you furnished years ago."

"Aside from the jewelry and the money, the only other things of value were several pieces of furniture and some silver," she said. "I'm sure they were easy to sell or, in the case of the silver, melt down."

"We'll be in touch if other things turn up. Thank you for today."

"Are we done?"

"Absolutely. I hope you and your family have a pleasant afternoon and evening," he said, smiling as he tucked a small notepad in his pocket.

"You too," she said. She stepped out of the dark, dank space and took a deep breath, the first she'd taken since she'd entered the apartment.

*****

As soon as the limo door closed, Harriet said, "I want to go home."

"I can have the plane ready in an hour," Spark said.

"I mean home, home," she said, looking over at her mother.

"Of course, sweetheart. We can leave as soon as you want," Helen said.

The others stared but said nothing. Harriet looked around at the kind gazes of their friends. "Sorry, that sounded very rude and abrupt, didn't it?" Her green eyes were soft as she met Kyle's.

Spark reached back and patted her hand. "Not a bit of it, darlin'. You've been through hell and back. Let's get you back to Saguaro, and you can make plans."

"Thank you, Spark. You've all been so kind and caring. I don't want you to think that I'm not incredibly grateful." As she spoke, she reached over, grasped Kyle's hand, and squeezed it.

"Let's everyone pack. I'll order lunches for the plane, and we can head to the airfield at one. Does that suit everyone?" Spark said.

"Thank you, dear Spark," Helen said, smiling at him.

CHAPTER 28

Kyle sensed that Harriet had closed down, and he was literally going crazy. When they reached the airport, he pulled her aside. "Are you okay? Can we talk?"

"Not now," she said, placing a hand on his wrist. "Maybe later, when we're back at Spark's? I don't want to talk to anyone right now, even you." She smiled and extracted her hand. "I'm okay, really I am. Just ready to get back to reality, I guess."

With those words, Harriet walked onto the plane and took a seat beside her mother. Before anyone could speak to her, she closed her eyes and slept. Helen leaned forward and whispered to Kyle seated just ahead beside Aria. "She does this sometimes. Better to let her sleep it off."

After landing, the group dispersed toward vehicles in Grenville. Harriet sensed Kyle beside her and turned to him. "I'm gonna ride back with Spark and the others."

"Harriet, wait," he said, reaching out to take her hand.

She gazed at him with sad eyes. This wonderful man who had helped her hold on to sanity. "I know I'm acting like a crazy person. I'm sorry. Can you give me a few hours? Maybe we could take a walk after dinner, if you're free?"

"Of course, babe, whatever you need. What time?"

"Around eight?"

"I'll be there."

The others gave him sympathetic looks but said nothing as he waved and headed for his truck left for him earlier by his brothers.

*****

Confused and worried, Kyle spent the thirty-minute drive to Morgan's Run thinking about the events of the past few days. First there was Harriet's erratic behavior, understandable under the circumstances, but he was also trying to sort out his feelings for Helen's fragile, wounded daughter. He cared about her, of that there was no doubt. *But do I love her, or was I just trying to get her through the horror show of facing Arthur Greene?*

He'd had serious relationships before, but nothing quite like this. In truth, his style wasn't exactly love 'em and leave 'em, but he had always managed to stay somewhat detached. Not this time. *You've jumped into the deep end here, buddy.* Much as the idea of her leaving distressed him, he wasn't at all sure what he wanted in regard to Harriet. *There's the sex—oh my God, the sex—but there's also something more. This is uncharted territory,* he thought as he drove through the ranch gates and up the drive to the Big House. *I really have to move out of here to my own place,* he thought, taking the porch steps two at a time.

As Kyle tried to sneak in the front door and up the stairs, his mother called, "Hi, honey! Dad's out on the terrace. Come join us for a drink."

"Be right down," he said. *And on to the Inquisition!*

"Hey, son, welcome back," Ben Senior said as Kyle stepped onto the terrace, a cold bottle of Desert Amber in hand. It was a glorious Valley evening, with a cool breeze and clear sky, just a hint of rosy hue to the west.

"Thanks, Dad. Can I get you a fresh one?"

Leonora shook her head. "No, you cannot. Chester has restricted him to one cocktail a night." She referred to Chester Black, her husband's physician and friend.

Ben Senior winked at his son. "She's no fun."

"So?" Leonora said.

"So, I'm back."

"How'd it go?" his father asked.

"I'm sure it felt worse than having a root canal to Harriet, but she held up great. Looks like they'll nail the bastard on a bunch of charges."

"Hallelujah!" Ben Senior said. "Your gal must be so relieved. Helen too."

"Not sure she's my gal, but yes, I'm sure it's a big relief. Closes an ugly chapter."

Leonora narrowed her gaze, regarding her son. "So how do things stand with you and Harriet? You've been seeing so much of each other."

"She apparently wants to leave Saguaro immediately."

Leonora's eyes widened. "But they weren't scheduled to go home until next week. Oh, honey, what's happened?"

"Nothing. Just court, I guess. Testifying and all. I think it rattled her. She wants to get back to the familiar and a sense of normalcy."

"Of course she does," his father said.

Leonora gave her husband a dismissive wave. "Hush, now. Something else must be up."

"Mom, can we not do this right now?" he asked, suddenly weary. "I'm going over there later. I'll know more then."

"Oh, honey, of course. You must be starved! I'll check with Carmela about dinner."

When she disappeared, Kyle turned to his father. "Got any advice while she's out of the room?"

"She's just worried. You know your mom. My advice is listen, follow that big heart of yours, and you'll figure it out."

"You have more faith in me than I do."

"I don't know Harriet, but I know Helen pretty well. She's a keeper. An amazing woman who went through hell and has come out the other end strong, kind, and beautiful. She's given those girls of hers lots of love too."

"Okay, you two!" Leonora called. "Come on, dinner's ready."

The three sat, and Carmela served her colorful Southwest chopped salad and ranch-style individual pizzas, healthy recipes she had developed in response to Ben Senior's heart issues. The thin-crust pizza had a cauliflower crust and was topped with chicken, Carmela's salsa, and a thin sprinkling of local cheese. The salad brimmed with ranch produce—cabbages in bright shades of green and red, red peppers, celery, kohlrabi, and jicama—and was lightly tossed with a piquant lime dressing.

"This is incredible, Carm," Kyle said, taking a bite of pizza. Carmela smiled and disappeared into the kitchen.

"You guys have really spoiled me. I'll miss Carmela's cooking when I move to my own place."

"Which you do not have to do. Ever," his mother said. "I'm gonna bring Ruthie and Harley some of this salad tomorrow. I'm not sure she appreciates what can be done with the farm's incredible variety of produce."

"Yes, I do. It's time," Kyle said, helping himself to two more slices of pizza.

"Where're you thinkin', son?" his father asked. "You know Tom Jacobi's house is near complete," he said, referring to Harley's assistant as trainer and manager of Valley Stables. "And Kevin's crew has started on the second house for the resident veterinarian."

"You should give that to Gus Casey. With his two kids and all, he needs it more than I do," Kyle said, referring to Jacobi's assistant who would be overseeing most of the training.

"Gus is all settled in town," his mother said.

"In a house that's way too small. I've seen it."

"Thanks, son. I'll talk with Spark and Harley," Ben Senior said. "Cute kids, those Caseys. Must be hard without a momma. They seem to like the gang over the Cottage," he added, referring to the ranch's day care.

"Of course they do! Polly and Lynn are amazing," Leonora said, taking a sip of her white wine. "Now, about this evening, honey."

"There's nothing about this evening that we need to discuss," he said, turning to his father, eyes pleading.

"Now, Nora, let the boy be."

Ignoring her husband, Leonora pressed on. "She's had a very troubled past, honey. I know you're a good, caring soul, but that's a lot to take on."

"Mom, I know you're trying to help, but please stop. I know about Harriet's past. She's strong."

"Helen Winthrop's marriage was extremely abusive."

"Mom…"

"Nora, let's leave it."

"Her daughters witnessed things no child should ever see."

Kyle stood up. "Mom, I know you mean well, but this conversation is over. I'm gonna skip dessert."

"Honey, wait. As a very young child, Harriet witnessed her mother being beaten and raped. On more than one occasion."

"Nora, that's enough!"

As he moved to leave, she grabbed Kyle's hand. "It was deeply traumatic! She probably doesn't even have conscious memory of some of it."

Kyle wriggled out of her grasp. "Night," he said quietly.

As he walked out, he heard his father say, "Enough, honey. He's a grown man."

"Who's stepped into a madhouse. I'm only thinking of him."

As Kyle shut the door to his room, her words echoed. He knew the probable reasons Harriet had been hiding in her closet, but hearing them from his usually prim and proper mother was shocking. He buried his head in his hands and thought not for the first time, *What the hell have I walked into? And how can I leave her alone?*

CHAPTER 29

Harriet packed the last of her things, then lay on the bed, closing her eyes. It had been a quiet dinner, just Helen, Spark, and herself. He had invited Aria to join them, but she had a migraine, and after laying out the dinner buffet style in the kitchen, she retreated to her apartment. A soft knock and her mother stepped in.

"All packed?" Helen sat at the end of the bed.

"Yup. You?"

"Almost."

"Mum, I'm sorry about cutting the trip short. I wish you'd consider staying on. I know Spark wants you to."

"I'm ready too," she said quietly. "You know what a recluse I am, and this is a busy place. It will be good to get home to familiar routines."

"Have you heard from the yarners?"

"Just Frankie. She emailed yesterday to check on us."

"You'll have plenty of tales to tell at the next meeting."

"They love to hear about the Wild West."

"And your screwed-up daughter."

"Harriet, you know I never talk about you or your sisters."

Harriet raised an eyebrow, smiling at her. "Not even to Frankie?"

"Well, Frankie and I do confide in each other, that's true. But nothing ever goes further."

"You should bring Frankie out here on one of your trips. They'd love her and she them."

"Don't think I haven't asked, but she's always busy, between the glasswork and her investigating."

The doorbell rang, and Harriet sat up. "That will be Kyle."

"Oh?"

"We're going for a walk. To say goodbye."

"Are you sure?"

"Yes," she said, grabbing a sweater hanging on a ladderback chair. "I won't be too long."

"He really cares about you, sweetheart."

Harriet gazed down at her mother's eyes, sad but resigned. "I know, and I care about him, but this was no more than a vacation fling."

"How do you know that?"

"Because it has to be. Don't wait up. I'll see you at breakfast. What time does Spark think we should leave?"

"By eight." Spark had insisted his plane could fly them home and they could save their refundable return tickets for their next trip. The plane and pilot would be standing by in Grenville.

"Night, Mum," she said, stooping to kiss Helen's cheek.

"Night, sweetheart. I love you."

"Me too, you," she said, closing the door behind her.

*****

"Nice night," Kyle said as they started down a well-worn path at the edge of Spark's property. A cart path of long standing, it was still used by riders heading for the western mountains. About a half mile along, the right fork branched off heading west. The left fork turned south on a semicircle that bordered Spark's land and ended up two miles later at the end of his driveway.

"Yes, it is," she said, tying her sweater around her waist. She wore jeans, sneakers, and a long-sleeved rose-colored jersey. He too was in jeans, a ranch T-shirt, hiking boots, and a worn gray Stetson that she hadn't seen before. *Gorgeous as always*, she thought. Her heart beat faster at his nearness, and she steeled herself for what was to come.

They walked in silence for several minutes. Finally, he said, "Not sure how long you want to go, but this loops around and comes back to Spark's in a couple of miles."

"That's perfect," she said. "Looks like we've got an hour at least before sunset."

"So you're really going?" he asked, pushing his hat back off his brow.

"Yes," she said quietly, eyes lowered.

"What changed your mind? About staying, I mean?"

"I need familiar ground. This has all been amazing. Every minute. Well… except the time in court. I feel like I've been in a dream. You and me, this amazing place, all the people… I come from a small town, but nothing like this. I think it might be time for me to wake up and go home. Back to reality."

"So, you and me? Just a dream?"

"No… Yes… I don't know, Kyle." She paused and turned to face him. "The last thing I want to do is hurt or offend you. You've been nothing but kind, loving, and incredibly supportive. And so much more."

His dark eyes flashed fire and hurt. "A diversion? Stress relief? Roll in the hay?"

"No, nothing like that!" She stared at him, wondering what to say. *Don't lead him on. Stay strong!* "I just need to get home and, to use a psycho-babble term, process. I'm long overdue to see my therapist."

He took her hands, eyes holding hers. "I won't push you, Harriet. I care about you. I'm in love with you, but I won't pressure you. In truth, I don't know what the hell I'm doing either, but I was kinda hoping we'd figure things out together. Hoping we'd have more time."

Harriet withdrew her hands and began walking. "I know. I'm sorry. This is just something I have to do."

They walked for most of the loop, the silence between them screaming by the time they reached the gates of Spark's property. As they headed up the drive in the growing twilight, he said, "Come this way. We can circle the house, and then I'll let you go."

As they came around the back of the biggest barn, there were four benches lined against the north wall. "Just for a minute," he said, sitting and patting the bench beside him.

"Before we say good night, can you answer me one question?" he asked.

"I'll try."

"Has this…us…been a vacation fling?"

Aghast, Harriet stared at him. "Absolutely not. You know it hasn't."

"Then what?"

"Excuse me?"

"Then what's it been?"

Harriet swallowed hard. It was all she could do to stop herself from flinging herself into his arms and losing herself in his warm, embracing love. "It's been the most amazing time in my life."

"Then what's there to process?"

"Everything. The trial, seeing Louis again, you and me. A romance with one of the infamous Morgan boys. The whole thing."

"If you haven't noticed, I'm the only one of the infamous Morgan boys who's not settled down with the love of his life."

"Is that what you want? To settle down?"

"I don't know."

"Exactly," she said. "I've got to go in."

"Harriet, give me a break!" he said, grabbing hold of her hand as she stood. "We've known each other for less than a minute. I'm crazy about you, but I've never even considered what settling down means, let alone doing it."

She stooped, placing gentle fingers on either side of his handsome, angular face. "Kyle, you are the love of my life, but I can't do this right now. I need to go home and get my bearings. I'm sorry."

She kissed him softly. "Say goodbye to Misty for me, and take good care of her."

Before he could stop her, Harriet ran to the house and disappeared inside. Her heart raced as she closed the door, then she crumpled inside, a sobbing heap.

"Hey, little gal," Spark said, stepping into the dimly lit foyer. "Come have a nightcap with an old man who's gonna miss you and your mom."

Harriet wiped her eyes and followed him into his study. "You think I'm crazy, don't you?" she asked as he handed her a snifter of brandy.

"Nope, just confused. It's been a tumultuous visit, hasn't it?"

She smiled at him. It wasn't like Spark to use words like tumultuous. "Something like that."

"He's a good kid, Kyle Morgan."

"Kid?"

He grinned. "Man. Not easy following in the footsteps of his older brothers. Still seems like a kid to me. Ruthie too."

"He's a wonderful man," she said, taking a sip of brandy, which burned the back of her throat.

"Yep. Comes from the best family in the world."

"What about yours?"

He grinned wider. "We're all one family, darlin'."

"I love him, Spark. I do, but we jumped into this so fast. Then the whole Louis thing. You know something? I can say his name now. He's lost his power over me."

"So the jaunt to California might've been worth it in some small way?"

"Yes, I think so. Have you got any sage advice for me on this next jaunt?"

Spark gazed at her with kind, wise eyes. "I'm an ole hound dog, darlin'. I know how to make money and I live well, but I can't offer much advice in matters of the heart. I was married to my Patsy for over half my life. She was the love of my life. No one will ever touch that. I will say that I never thought I could live without her, but humans are stronger than we look. I've managed to keep goin' without my sweet girl for our kids, my friends, and all my loyal, honest employees. It's been a grand ride. You go home, get your bearings, see how you feel. The right way'll come to you. It always does."

"Thanks, Spark," she said, standing.

He stood, and they embraced.

"Mom and I are so lucky to have you as a dear friend."

"Darlin', the luck is all mine. Get a good night's sleep now."

CHAPTER 30

"What the hell is wrong with him?" Harley Langdon asked as he and Tom Jacobi leaned against a fence rail outside the stables. "He's been bouncing around the barn like a ping-pong ball."

"I believe it has something to do with a certain lady who just flew the coop. At least that's the news from the ranch grapevine," Jacobi said, chewing on a piece of straw. The handsome farm manager had heard about Harriet and Helen's departure from Nick Parker, who had come from the ranch to help with one of the skittish thoroughbreds.

"Where's Parker now?"

"Already on his way back to Morgan's Run."

"Great. I've two Morgans drivin' me crazy today. My wife's been calling and texting every other minute with some crisis, and now her brother. Christ, where the hell's Patty?"

"In town getting supplies."

"I need Oscar out on the east run. Can you handle that? I'll go grab my idiot brother-in-law. Why didn't he just give in to the inevitable and marry the woman?"

Jacobi smiled, watching his boss disappear, headed for the veterinary examining rooms.

Harley stepped into the first room and found Kyle was unpacking boxes and storing medicines and supplies. When he spied Harley, he put up his hand, "Don't start! I'm busy. I've examined Oscar, and he's fine. Just settling in jitters. I've gotta finish this and head back to the ranch to check on Misty."

Harley made a T shape with his hands. "Time out, buddy. Stop what you're doing and talk to me."

"Nothing to say."

"Why didn't you check on Misty this morning before you came here?"

"No time."

"Hasn't been a problem before today."

Kyle stopped and glared at his brother-in-law. Truth was, his brother Ben's friend had always intimidated him growing up, and the edge still lingered. "What do you want, Harley? You gonna fire me? Go ahead."

Harley raised both hands in surrender. "All right, all right, buddy. But if you won't talk to me, find someone. Please, for all our sakes. This is a critical time. We've got inspectors coming and all kinds of shit goin' on. Patty's great, but she needs supervision. Tom and Gus can't do the medical stuff, nor can I or any of the trainers."

Kyle paused, hands on hips, head lowered. "I'm a complete horse's ass, aren't I?"

"Love does that to you, buddy."

"I don't know how to function knowing she's three thousand miles away."

Harley raised an eyebrow. "Technically, she's probably only a thousand or two at this point. Still in the air, I expect?"

"What the hell am I gonna do?"

"The last of the Morgan boys fallen."

"Ha-ha."

"You'll get over it, but not by throwing shit all over the place. Is there any rhyme or reason to what you've been doing in here?"

Kyle grinned. "Hell no."

"Then get the hell outta here. Go check on Misty, then go home. Talk to your dad, take a ride, put some sweat in with my wife and Beth, anything to get your mind off this. Patty can straighten up here, and you two can talk later. *Comprende?*"

"That's fucked up. I belong here."

"I've got Ned Williams comin' out this afternoon. I can pull him into the mix."

"That's not fair to you or Ned."

"We'll survive. Now get the hell outta here and don't come back till she's out of your system."

"Christmas?"

"Tomorrow morning for sure, but try to meet with Patty later, okay? I can send her to the ranch."

"I'll call her. Thanks, Harl."

As Kyle drove his truck down the long Valley Stables drive, he wondered if he was indeed going crazy. *I can't see her. I can't touch her. What the hell am I gonna do?*

As he drove through town, he decided to stop at the café for a coffee. As he pushed open the door, Dara Littlefield, Maggie's friend, came out, a large iced tea in one hand.

"Well, well, well, Kyle Morgan. I heard you were back in town."

"Dara, hi. Yeah, for many moons. I'm resident vet out at Valley Stables."

"Maggie told me something about that. You still have the Morgan smile and looks, I see. Not fair that you guys are so gorgeous. It seems like forever since I've seen you."

"Pretty much." *Since Maggie and Ben's wedding, to be exact, when I flirted shamelessly with you, then skipped town.*

"So, have you got time to sit and catch up?"

"Well, I…don't," he said, then shrugged, "Why not? Let me grab a coffee, and I'll be right out."

They strolled across the street to the town green and sat on a bench in the shade.

"So, what's new with the only remaining bachelor Morgan?"

"Technically, Robbie's not married."

Dara batted her eyelashes, pale blue eyes shining with interest. She was pretty in a well-scrubbed way. Her strawberry-blonde hair was straight and fell to her shoulders. Dara had flawless skin. Her gingham blouse matched her eyes, and her denim capris looked like pedal pushers from the last century. "Yeah, but he and Hope might as well be. They're so cute together. They live in my building, you know. Three doors down." More eyelash batting.

"Yeah?"

"You know, I should be mad at you," she said, giving him a playful swat. "You had my number and never called."

"Sorry, it was a crazy time with Emma's rehab and all. What're you up to these days?"

"I work at the bank. Not sure for how long, but it's an income."

"Great."

"So what about now?" she said.

"Excuse me?"

"Since you've settled back here, what about calling me now?"

Kyle smiled. "I'm kind of seeing someone."

"Kind of?"

"She lives in Massachusetts."

"How's that working out?"

"We'll see."

"Well, give me a call, if you're free or just want to go out, no strings. Maggie has my numbers. Or you can stop by when you're visiting your brother." She stood. "Duty calls. Lunch break over."

"Good to see you, Dara."

"You too. Remember, sweetie. No strings, and I'll never tell." She winked, then turned away to sashay down the sidewalk toward Valley Bank.

Kyle grinned watching her. *Just what I need.*

CHAPTER 31

When they arrived at the beach house, Harriet carried her mother's bags to the bedroom.

"Why don't you stay the night, sweetheart?"

"Thanks, Mum, but I want to get home. Can I do anything for you before I go?"

"Not unless you'd like to have a cup of tea or something to eat before you go?"

"I'm good, thanks. Spark's crew takes 'airplane food' to a whole new level. I'm still stuffed."

Helen laughed. "Me too! If they'd brought out one more platter of food, I'd have popped."

Harriet sat beside her mother on the four-poster adorned with a brightly patterned quilt. "You okay, Mum? I know you'd rather have stayed with Spark awhile longer."

"I'm fine."

"You like him, don't you?"

"Yes. As a friend. That's it. He had his Patsy and I had Tim for a brief moment in time. Those loves will always overshadow the rest."

"But could you see more happening with Spark?"

"No, sweetie. This is my home, and he clearly loves the Valley. So...we enjoy our lovely visits."

"Is he coming east sometime soon?"

"Probably not with the new thoroughbred venture. Maybe next summer."

"He's a lovely man."

Helen gazed at her, eyes soft. "Yes, he is. How about you, honey? Are you okay?"

"Well, I haven't vomited or binged, and my arms are scratch-free, so that's something. I'll be glad to check in with Elise. I have an appointment Monday. You know, last night, I was surprised to admit to Spark that the court day may have done me some good. Facing my demons, maybe? Louis looked awful, didn't he?"

"To tell you the truth, I barely glanced at him, but he's an awful man, and evil often doesn't age well."

"Well, I'd better head out. Thanks for inviting me on the trip and for agreeing to come home early."

"I'm happy to be home, sweetheart. Although I will miss being waited on hand and foot." She chuckled as she stood to see Harriet out. They hugged at the door, and both waved as Harriet drove off.

*****

The house was quiet as Harriet stepped in and climbed to her second-floor bedroom. The little cottage at the edge of campus had been her home since she'd moved out of the dorms five years earlier. Lately, she'd been contemplating buying a house of her own, but the simple cottage served her purposes beautifully, though a bit drafty and worn. She breathed in the familiar smells of lemon, dust, and the sea as she moved about unpacking and tidying up. After the palatial accommodations at Spark's and the vivid colors of the valley landscape, her world seemed a bit drab and lifeless. She settled in her rocker, gazed out at the fields, and sighed. *My life is drab and lifeless without him.*

The phone's ring jarred her back to the present, and she answered, "Hello?"

"Hi, sis, you're back," Hazel said, her voice cheerful as always. "How was it?"

"Complicated. Beautiful, amazing, unsettling, and complicated."

"Ooh, sounds interesting. I'm coming down to see Mum tomorrow. Let's do something. A walk or dinner? Anything."

"Are you spending the night?"

"Maybe."

"Want to stay here?"

"I was hoping you'd ask. Mum's busy with the Darn Yarners tomorrow night. Why don't I visit with her, do some errands in the Cove, and plan to get to you about five-ish. Does that sound okay?"

"You never have to wait for me to ask, you know. I love having you anytime. See you soon, then."

A part of Harriet wanted to be alone to "process" and get her bearings, but another part of her craved the comforting presence of loved ones. *Hazel's visit might be just what I need.* She unpacked her small suitcase, brewed a cup of tea, and sat back by the window, gazing out at the school's playing fields, deserted now. It was a warm night, but she shivered, wondering if she'd ever be warm again. Later, as she plugged her cell into its charger, she noticed a text. It was from Kyle.

Hey, just checking to see if you made it home safely.

Harriet replied: *We did.*

Miss you, came back almost immediately.

Harriet stared at her phone for a long while. *Don't lead him on. Keep things friendly!* Finally, she texted, "Night, take care," and turned off the phone. *What's the matter with me?* she thought as she drifted off to sleep.

*****

"Bad news, bro?" Ben Morgan asked as he watched his youngest brother slip his cell phone back in his jeans.

"I blew it," Kyle said. He plunked down on a bench outside the Valley Stables barn.

"I heard they left," Ben said, sitting down beside him. "Bummer when you guys were connecting, right?"

"How the hell do I know? What are you doin' over here anyway?"

"Haven't you heard? Another pack trip comin' up. I'm here to persuade your boss to come with me."

"With a new baby and this place just gearing up?"

"Yep. Mom's over with Charlotte every five minutes, and Tom and Gus have this place running like a well-oiled machine. Besides, there's not a whole heck of a lot to do at this stage."

"Says you."

"You did a great job with Misty, by the way. Maggie says she's healing nicely. That sling contraption was pretty slick."

"Yeah, it worked pretty good. If you're looking for your partner in crime, he's out by the north track. I'll walk out with you."

The two brothers strolled across the green expanse to a pristine mile-and-a-half track where a rider circled on a beautiful black horse.

"So you like her, Helen's daughter?"

"Harriet? Yeah, I like her. I love her."

"Oh boy—my gadabout little brother has finally been bitten by the love bug."

"Ha-ha."

"Did you tell her?"

"Yup."

"And?"

"And she immediately flew across the country as far away as she could get from me."

"Was that the reason she hightailed it?"

"No... Maybe... Who the hell knows. She says it was all too much, too soon."

"You could go after her. It worked for Sammy," he said, referring to their brother who had followed his now wife, Rose, to Maryland, where he proposed.

"I can't do that. After all the shit she's been through, she deserves the space to figure out what she wants."

"Here's my man," Ben said as they came to stand next to Harley.

Harley leaned against the fence. He nodded, still watching horse and rider. "She's a beauty, isn't she?"

"I'll take Rowdy any day," Ben said. "And speaking of my trusty steed, he and I need you along when we take the next trip. Ten days, ten celebs. We're gearing up now, and they arrive tomorrow for orientation, then we head out at the end of the week. I'm taking Parker. With Misty out of commission, both Friesians are both coming, and he's the best with them, but we need a third leader, buddy."

"You gotta be kidding. We're out straight here," Harley said.

Kyle grinned. "Told you."

"Come on, man. How many times have I gotten you out of a jam?"

"Not as many as I have you," Harley said, gazing back at horse and rider.

"You're the boss. Delegate."

"Sorry, man, there's no way I can go. Ask Robbie."

"He's busy, and he's not a strong enough rider for ten days on rough terrain. They want to follow the Ridge on the way back, and I'm not takin' Robbie up there.""

"I'll go," Kyle said. "I can handle it, and it wouldn't hurt to have a vet along."

"What to hand out the panty hose?" Ben said.

"Ha, ha," Kyle said, "Although don't knock the medical benefits of panty hose on the trail."

"Problem solved," Harley said. "Sorry guys, gotta run." With that, the manager of Valley Stables headed off toward the main barn.

Ben eyed his brother. "Are you sure about this?"

"Yup. Be good practice for Patty. I still have time to get things set up for her. You don't need me for orientation, do you?"

"Probably not. Mag and Jeb can help us, but we need you hobnobbin' at the Welcome Reception tomorrow night."

"Can't wait."

"Okay, but don't say I didn't warn you."

CHAPTER 32

Harriet loved the twenty-minute drive from campus to Horseshoe Crab Cove, where her mother lived. Elise Nolan, her therapist, had her office above Village Books, the greatest bookstore in the world, in Harriet's opinion. After running a mail-order children's book company for years, Lucy, her sister, now managed the children's room and continued to operate her online business from there.

After driving through fields and woods, she crested the hill and the Cove lay before her with its kidney shaped peninsula, tiny town, and beautiful harbor. If she had time, Harriet frequently stopped at the overlook to savor the view. She'd never found anything quite like it anywhere. Often, as a young teen, she had climbed to the overlook and sat gazing at the miles of vineyard to the east, shingled homes dotting the winding streets, the low fishery buildings near the docks, and farms that stretched to Lands' End and the bay beyond. She wished she could show this to Kyle. He loved New England and would surely appreciate this extraordinary place. *Someday*, she mused as she pulled back onto the road.

*****

"Good to see you, Harriet," Elise said, hugging her. "Want some tea?"
"Yes, that would be lovely."

The petite dark-haired therapist dressed in her usual leggings and jersey tunic collected two teacups and switched the kettle on. "I wasn't expecting you back so soon. Didn't we have an appointment in two weeks?"

"Change of plans," Harriet said, selecting a lavender honey tea bag and plunking it into one of the cups.

"Oh?"

"I saw Louis."

The usually calm and self-contained therapist almost dropped the steaming kettle as her dark eyes registered surprise. "How did that happen?"

As they fixed their tea, Harriet related the story of the past few days, ending with: "Somehow, awful as it was, seeing him again seems to have released me from his hold."

"Well, that's wonderful news," Elise said, curling her long, thin legs under her in the overstuffed chair. Elise was a serious runner who often jogged the village loop trail. She and Harriet had even had a few therapy sessions jogging, but Elise was twenty-six and a marathon runner. Harriet always felt like she slowed her down.

"Yes, I can say his name now. Did you notice?"

"Sure did. I'm glad you had your support team with you. Tell me about them. More specifically, tell me about Kyle."

Harriet gulped her tea, then proceeded to describe her love affair with the youngest Morgan son. Finally, she said, "He's wonderful. Six years younger than I am."

"Is that a problem?"

"Not for me, and he doesn't seem to care."

"So why *did* you come back early?"

"Honestly, I don't know. I felt out of control. Like I might fall off the precipice again, you know?"

"Even though you say Mr. Carrington or Greene has lost his hold on you?"

"This isn't about Louis. It's about me and what could happen."

"Such as?"

"My heart getting smashed into a million pieces. What I feel for him is nothing like what I've ever felt for any man, Louis or otherwise. If he broke things off, I'm not sure I could come back."

"Was he threatening to break things off?"

"No, just the opposite, but he's never had a long-term relationship."

"Perhaps he's never had a person he cares for as he does you. Do you love this man?"

"Yes," Harriet said, surprised that the word came so easily.

"Then this is about you, Harriet, not Kyle Morgan. Whatever you do, it should be what *you* want. You're in control. If he should ride off into the sunset, which, from what you've told me, is unlikely, you will know that the decision to pursue the relationship or not was yours and yours alone. That's the most important thing."

They talked awhile longer, then Elise said, "So what is your plan for tonight?"

"I think I'll call him."

"Good. See how that goes, and we'll talk tomorrow."

"How about calling around ten?"

The two hugged, and Harriet departed, feeling calm and peaceful for the first time since she said goodbye to Kyle.

*****

Kyle headed into town after work, intending to eat at Gracie's. He wasn't up to another one of his mother's interrogations. She'd been at him nonstop since Harriet left. As he walked into the diner, a voice called from the back booth. "Yoo-hoo! We meet again!"

Dara Littlefield waved as her redheaded companion turned her head to see the object of her friend's effusive greeting. Kyle nodded, hoping to forestall further conversation. *No such luck.* Dara hopped up and came to meet him. "Join us, won't you? Josie and I would love it."

"Thanks, but I'm meeting someone," he said, hating to lie but in no mood for small talk.

"You naughty boy. I told you to call me."

"It's been a busy few days."

"How's the Massachusetts romance?"

She probably knows damn well how my nonromance is going, he thought, forcing a smile. "I think your friend's waitin' on you."

She waved her hand dismissively. "I've waited on Josie plenty of times."

"Well, I'll let you get back to your dinner."

"And you to your imaginary friend?"

"Not sure what's keeping him."

"Okay, okay, I can take a hint. If you're ever back on the market, sugar, give me a ring-a-ling." With a wink, she sashayed off, swaying her flat, nondescript ass.

Kyle slid onto a stool just as Gracie emerged from the kitchen. "Hey, handsome, what's eating you?"

"Don't start, Gracie, please. I'll have tonight's fish special, a salad, and a chocolate shake."

"Trouble in paradise?"

He gave her a sheepish grin. "Gracie, please. Not tonight. By the way, you've got a bit of fusilli sticking to your head."

"Tonight's pasta special," she said, waving over her shoulder as she disappeared.

CHAPTER 33

"Can't hide from me forever," his mother called as Kyle tiptoed through the foyer on his way to the stairs. "Come have a nightcap, honey."

Sighing, Kyle veered his course and stepped into the living room, finding both parents. His father gave him a sympathetic nod. "Want a beer, son?"

"Why not," he said. "I'll get it."

When Kyle returned from the kitchen, both parents' eyes were trained on him. Before either could speak, he said, "Mom, Dad, I'm fine, really. No need to belabor this. She's gone, I'm busy, and that's that."

"We heard you're goin' on the pack trip with your brother," Ben Senior said.

"Yup."

"Did you run that by Harley first?"

"He's fine with it, and Patty can take care of the clinic."

Leonora stared at him. "It's ten days, honey. You haven't ridden in a while."

"He's the best rider of the family with the exception of his baby sister."

"Even so."

"You're not taking my baby, are you?" his mother asked.

"Nope."

"How's her leg doing?" she asked.

Kyle looked up. "You know about that?"

She waved her hand. "This is Morgan's Run, honey. No secrets here. Took little Benny down to the stables last week, and my poor baby was swinging from the rafters like a big ole white spider."

"Sorry, Mom, I meant to tell you. She's gonna be fine."

"Of course she is, with the best vet in the world lookin' after her."

"It was an accident."

"That's what Ned told us," his father said.

"So you've talked to Ned too?"

"She's been my baby for many years, darlin'. I check on her every day."

"Why didn't you say something?" Kyle asked.

"We knew you had your reasons for keeping it from us, and we knew you were handling it," his father said.

"Thanks." Kyle leaned back in his chair and shut his eyes.

"So? Have you spoken to her?" Leonora asked.

"Yeah, I speak to her, but she's not much of a talker."

"Oh, when?"

"At the barn. We had a good ole chat while I was changing her bandage."

"Ha-ha. You know I'm not talking about Misty."

"No, I haven't spoken to Harriet. I'm going to give her the space she needs. Maybe in a week or two."

"Is that wise?"

"Who knows, but that's what I'm doin'. Now I'm beat, so I'm goin' to bed."

"Don't forget tomorrow night's reception," his father said.

"I'll be there," Kyle said, turning away.

CHAPTER 34

Harriet had planned to call Kyle, but Hazel changed her plans and arrived a day earlier than expected. After a long walk, the sisters decided to ride into town and grab lobster rolls for a beach picnic. Harriet packed a basket with a blanket, wine, glasses, napkins, and chips. They stopped at the Cove Restaurant to pick up their dinner, then headed to the Point, an outcropping at the peninsula's southern tip. The village of Horseshoe Crab Cove was situated at the northern end of a long, curving peninsula. The eastern side of the peninsula was mostly open fields leading to a farm and ranch, the outermost point known as Land's End. The western shore was lined with cottages as well as the marina and fishery. At the end of the western side lay the point, a large rock formation known to the locals as the Nubble. A favorite picnic spot of the Winthrop sisters growing up, they still loved to climb the Nubble and gaze out to sea at sunset .

"Perfect night for it," Hazel said as they climbed the steep path leading to open grassy spots at the top.

Harriet nodded, following her nimble-footed sister.

The top was deserted tonight except for a few fishermen at the far end. They selected a spot, spread the blanket, and settled in. "Oh, I've missed this!" Hazel sighed, taking a sip of the cool crisp Chardonnay.

"Yes, it's lovely, isn't it?" Harriet said, leaning back. *Too bad I left my heart three thousand miles away.*

"So? Are you gonna tell me about it?" Hazel asked, her dark eyes sparkling with curiosity.

"About what?"

"About the guy."

"Mother told you?"

"No, but look at you. You're working overtime to be cheerful, sis, but let's face it, you're a wreck."

"That obvious, huh?"

"Was the sex good?"

"Hazel!"

"You can't hide anything from me, bubby. I can see right through you. You've been fucked and fucked well, honey."

"Hazel!"

"You gonna tell me, or am I gonna continue with this line of questioning?"

"It was transformative. Life-altering."

"That sounds extremely promising."

"It's complicated."

"By?"

"By the fact that we've known each other a week. He's never had a relationship that lasted more than a minute, and we live three thousand miles apart."

"Minor details," Hazel said, refilling both their glasses.

"No, they aren't."

"Do you love him?"

"Yes."

"Does he love you?"

"He thinks he does. That's the trouble."

"Are you listening to yourself? You love this man, he loves you, and you've been having life-altering sex. What's the problem here?"

"Dad, Louis, and my long sad history with men. What do I know about a healthy relationship? I'm hopeless."

"Harriet, Dad did a number on us, you especially. And Louis was just evil, but this guy sounds different. Tell me about him."

Harriet proceeded to describe the Valley and the Morgan family. Finally, she said, "After our childhood, it's amazing to be in the middle of such a loving family."

"We have and had a loving family, dear sister. Our mother. She is the most loving person alive."

"Who was beaten and abused for years by our father. What's to stop that happening to me?"

"Well, for one thing, your Kyle sounds like the opposite of Dad, and he's not related to our horror-show grandparents."

"I know, I know. Let's leave it for now, okay?"

"Fine, bubby, but my advice is to see where this leads. Relationships like you just described are few and far between."

"Seems to be the consensus opinion—you, Elise, Mom, and anyone who knows about the situation."

Hazel put her arm around her. "You mean anyone who loves you, bubby."

They walked back to the car in the twilight. Later, as they said good night, Harriet said, "I'll call him, maybe in a day or two."

"Good idea. Night, sis."

"Night."

CHAPTER 35

The reception in full swing, Ben, Kyle, and their father were cohosting, entertaining their ten guests. The pack trip would be three couples and four singles, three women and the brother of the wives. All were friends and four were actors who had an upcoming film project together. Four had gone on a previous trip. Damon Manning, a director, was returning with his wife, Samantha. She was an accomplished rider, and this time, she had brought her own horse, a tall, strong palomino. The third returnee was the actor Tom Harding, who brought his girlfriend, Madeline Ryan, a fellow actor. They were about to costar in a western action film together with two of the single women, Angie Lopez and Katherine "Kat" Doolittle. Kat's first big break was in the upcoming movie, and she was eager to get to know her costars, Angie, Tom, and Madeline. Damon's assistant, Willa Moody, was also onboard for her second pack trip. Kurt and Poppy Carter, friends of Damon and Samantha's brother Dickie Burns, rounded out the party.

"Quite a crew," Kyle said to his brother. "Where's Parker, anyway?"

Ben grinned. "Nick doesn't do social."

"This is gonna be a great ole time."

"Why do you think I needed reinforcements?" Ben said, nodding at Angie Lopez. "Hey, Ms. Lopez, lookin' good." And she did in a skintight jersey dress. Unlike Samantha Manning, who was wraith thin, Angie was all curves. "Let's hope that gorgeous ass knows how to stay in the saddle," he whispered to Kyle as the actress sidled up to the bar. "Lemme go talk to Manning, see if anyone needs riding practice tomorrow."

As Ben headed for the director, who stood with the Carter couple, Ben Senior came to stand beside Kyle. "Hey, son, how're you doin'?"

"Okay, Dad, what about you?"

"Same ole same ole."

"Before you ask, I haven't spoken to her, and I'm gonna give her the time and space she asked for. When I get back from the trip, we'll see."

"Sounds like a good plan."

"Dad, you know what you and Mom have is as rare as the Hope Diamond, don't you?"

"We're lucky, that's for sure. But look at your brothers and sisters. They've done pretty well. They're all happy with their mates."

"Yeah. Talk about lucky—Maggie, Lang, Rose, Hope, and Harley," Kyle said.

"All of 'em have had their share of bumps and rolls, your brothers and sisters and their spouses."

"That's not what's stopping me with Harriet."

"Oh?"

"She's scared shitless, Dad. The thought of a relationship with anyone is enough to unhinge her completely."

"Maybe that it's just what she needs? There's a lot of security in a loving partnership."

Father and son were suddenly interrupted by a gaggle of questions from their guests. Before they were dragged in separate directions, Kyle leaned over and said, "Thanks, Dad."

"You betcha, although there's no need for thanks. You've got it covered."

*****

The next day was a flurry of activity on the ranch with the pack trip and Emma's Dream, the camp founded by Maggie and Ben Morgan, was opening for its fourth summer, and they had their largest group of campers ever. They'd hired extra staff at the stables and at camp, and all had been trained and were ready to go. Emma's Dream brought handicapped children from all over the country to the ranch for two weeks of fun and horseback riding instruction.

Kyle spent the morning with Patty, getting things organized. In the afternoon, he headed to Morgan's Run to check and double-check provisions for the trip while Ben and Nick assessed the riders' ability and matched them with horses. Willa had requested Dandy, their neighbor Jaybo Dillon's horse. Dandy had been her mount on the previous trip, and the two had bonded. Tom Harding had requested Rowdy, the horse he'd ridden previously, but Rowdy was Ben's horse, so they paired the actor with Royal, Ben Senior's horse. Damon Manning would once again be on Whimsy, Martha Dillon's horse.

The following morning, Kyle arrived at the barn at five thirty. Nick was already there, as was Jeb Barnes, and they were in the process of saddling the horses and loading the three pack mules. Maggie was in the office checking supplies and trail maps.

"Mornin'," she called to her brother-in-law. "I'll be heading home soon to release your brother. I wanted to double-check everything. I'll take the kids to day care, then go to the Lodge to make sure everyone gets into the jeeps with all their gear."

"Good luck with that," Nick said, shaking his head. "Last time, we had to send a jeepful of crap back to the Lodge, then repack everything."

"Now, now, be kind. I should be the testy one. You guys are leaving us short-handed and short-horsed. Thank goodness for Jadie, Cocoa, and Sunny. I may try to borrow one more pony from the Masons."

"I thought those three were the only horses you guys used for camp," Kyle said.

"They are, but we have lessons too. I'm going to call Pat Wordell and Liz Baron, see if we can maybe use their horses in a pinch."

Jeb smiled, standing behind his boss. "You'd have better luck if Nickie asked them. They *love* Nickie."

"Barnes, that's right, hide behind Maggie's petticoats so I can't whip your ass," Nick said.

Maggie threw up her hands. "All right, you two. Enough. I haven't worn a petticoat. Ever." She gave Kyle a hug. "I'm heading home and leaving you to referee until Ben gets here. Have a safe and wonderful trip."

As they waited for Ben, the three men sat in the shade, speculating on what crises might arise on this trip. Kyle was only half listening, his thoughts on Harriet. He missed her terribly and wondered if it was a mistake to take off for ten days without calling. He'd shut off his cell phone and left it at home. Cell service was almost nonexistent where they were going. Besides, Ben would have a phone and probably everyone else in the party too.

CHAPTER 36

After a busy day with Hazel and her mom, Harriet sat in the quiet of her house, glad of the peace, but missing her sister's presence. Grounded and wise, Hazel always read her like a book. Too young to remember most of the horrors of life at Hill House, their youngest sister had been the least affected by the traumatic aspects of their childhood. Clara escaped in her music, and Lucy spent every possible moment with friends. So it was just Harriet and the baby present during Jud Winthop's drunken rages.

She fixed a cup of tea and sat in the living room in her favorite chair, gazing out at the starry night. In the silence, she could almost hear the ache of her heart. *This is ridiculous*, she thought. *You are torturing yourself for no reason.* She grabbed the phone and hit his number. Before long, his rich deep voice came on, asking her to leave a message. She wished she could listen to that voice forever. Not knowing what to say, she clicked off without leaving a message.

*****

"Great start, everybody," Ben called from the front of the trail, his fellow riders behind him. Nick rode five riders back, and Kyle brought up the rear. They were on a narrow stretch headed for the Painted Valley. Once they reached the crest and descended into the valley, the trail would open up, but now they were single file. With the exception of Angie Lopez and Katherine Doolittle, all were experienced riders. Willa Moody was a beginner, but she knew her horse, and they seemed settled and comfortable. Also, she had announced proudly, "I've been taking riding lessons."

The other two women had been given the gentlest, surest mounts, Raine and Tara, and so far, they had managed to stay in the saddle. Katherine rode just ahead of Kyle, and Angie was in the middle just behind Nick.

As they ascended, Kyle's horse, Blue, stepped lightly, sure-footed and nimble. Blue was a chestnut Trakehner, one of four of the warm-blooded breed recently acquired by Valley Stables. While the Trakehners would be part of the stable's dressage program, Blue was purchased for stud as his competing days were over. It had been generous and risky to loan him so soon after his arrival, but he and Kyle had already formed a bond, and the horse seemed calm and comfortable with him. Kyle patted him. "Good boy, Blue," he said as he watched Katherine just ahead. Tara was sure-footed and not easily spooked, but her rider was giving her mixed signals. One minute, Kat reined her tightly, the next, she let the reins hang loose. He wished he could pull alongside them, but there was no room. *Let us get to the top, and I'll straighten her out. Geez, ten days of this!*

When they crested the hill, Katherine simply abandoned the reins altogether. Disgusted, Kyle called, "Ms. Doolittle, grab your reins!"

Instead of following instructions, she turned in the saddle and promptly slid off into a small bush. "Geez," he said, dismounting and tying Blue to a small tree.

"Aah! Aah! Help!" she cried, caught in the thicket.

Kyle reached down and grabbed her hand. "You're lucky that wasn't a cactus. Up here, almost everything has sharp spikes or prickles."

"What do you call this? I'm covered with scratches!"

"Scratches, not puncture wounds. Come on, I have something for those."

When he returned with a jar of salve, he gazed down to where she'd fallen. "Oh, geez," he said, noticing the ground cover with its blue flowers all around the base of the bush.

"What?" she whined.

"You may have landed in some leadwort or plumbago. Funny to see it here. It's pretty rare."

She stared at him aghast. Her blonde hair, once in a smooth ponytail, was now askew, sticks and tufts of leaves stuck to it. "Why? Is it poisonous?"

"Could give you a rash. We'll see."

"What do you mean, we'll see? How bad of a rash?"

"Might be a bit painful, a few blisters. Then again, it might not be leadwort."

"Oh my God, I can't have a rash or blisters. I'm about to start filming for the biggest part of my career."

"You'll be fine in time for that. We're out for ten days." As he spoke, she extracted a packet of wet wipes from her pack and began wildly wiping every inch of her body, especially her face and neck. He didn't have the heart to tell her that the wipes would have little or no effect once the oil of the plant had touched her skin.

"I feel sick."

"Well, the good news is that we're only a couple of hours out. I can take you back, then catch up with the others. You can spend the next ten days at the Lodge having spa treatments."

The others had all but disappeared down the trail, but soon, his brother appeared. "What the hell's goin' on?" he asked, reining in Rowdy.

"Ms. Doolittle here had a bit of a fall, and she may have tangled with some leadwort," Kyle said, pointing to the bush.

"Looks like it," Ben said, dismounting. "Tough break. It can give you a nasty rash."

"I was just asking if she wanted me to take her back," Kyle said.

"Absolutely not!" Katherine said, hands on hips, face already reddening from a rash or from her frenzied wiping. "What would Damon and the others think? I'm on this god-awful trip to learn how to ride, so let's get a move on."

With a glance at his brother, Ben turned to her. "You know, we have great instructors back at the ranch. You'd probably learn more from them than you will up here."

"And let my fellow actors think I wimped out? Not a chance! Now help me up on this nag, and let's move it."

"With all due respect, Ms. Doolittle," Ben said.

"It's Kat, if you must know! Ms. Doolittle sounds like my grandmother."

Kyle watched his brother take a deep breath and marveled at his patience. In his earlier life, Ben Morgan was not known for being a patient man, but heart troubles had forced him to change his ways. Finally, he said, "Okay, Kat, listen to me. This is a ten-day trip, not a picnic in the park. It's gonna be rough. You'll be sleeping on the ground and saddle sore every day. I hope you followed instructions and wore your panty hose?"

"That's none of your goddamn business! Why would I want to make myself even hotter and more uncomfortable?"

"Anyway, as I was saying. This is not easy. My brother can take you back now and you can nurse your rash, gets lots of riding instruction, and enjoy the Lodge."

"Get me the hell back on that horse, now!" she said, eyes blazing.

Ben shrugged. "Okay, but if you're not wearing the panty hose we issued you, I'd strongly urge you to get 'em out and change quick. We won't peek."

"If I need them, I'll put them on tomorrow."

"Tomorrow will be too late."

"Get me on that nag. Now."

As Kyle lifted her, he said, "Her name is Tara, and I'd advise you to treat her with respect. She's no nag, and she's used to riders who know what they're doing. Don't let go of the reins again. Here, hold 'em like this, okay?"

She harrumphed, but he noticed that she held tight as they descended into the clearing where the others waited. By nightfall, she was covered with blisters and could barely walk.

CHAPTER 37

"You're taking the rear tomorrow, Parker," Kyle said as they prepared to bed down. "I need a break from Ms. Doolittle."

"Boss?" Nick asked, eyes on Ben.

"Only fair. I'd do it, but I need to stay in front. Besides, it gives Tabasco a break. He hates to be hemmed in." He referred to Maggie's enormous draft horse. No one but Nick dared ride him. They never used him for pack trips, but with camp and Misty laid up, Tabasco had been pressed into service. Gentle and sure-footed, he could still be intimidating to the other horses and riders.

Out of earshot of her fellow riders, Kat had complained nonstop since they stopped for the night and made camp. Her face, arms, and legs were covered with an angry, blistering rash, and she hobbled around camp, moaning about the insides of her thighs. She refused dinner and, after a glass of wine, she took two sleeping pills and disappeared into her tent.

One of the guides was always awake, and Ben volunteered to take the first shift. As Kyle headed for his bedroll at the east end of camp, he heard Angie talking to Willa. "I told her to wear the pantyhose, the stupid fool. She's a hurtin' cowgirl."

"Poor thing," Willa said.

"Poor thing my ass. If she's like this now, just imagine what she'll be like during filming."

Kyle smiled. He liked Willa. Damon's assistant was kind, generous, and quiet, three qualities he much admired. Her boss treated her like a doormat, his wife too, but Willa remained calm and cheerful no matter what they threw her way.

Sometime after midnight, his brother shook him awake. "Hey, bro, time to wake up." No sooner had he spoken than a cry came from the other side of camp.

"Help! Help! Wild boars!" It sounded like Samantha Manning's voice.

"Geez, now what?" Ben said, standing. The two brothers rushed toward the screams.

When they arrived at the Mannings' tent, they spied nine javelinas milling about, not the least bit intimidated by the proximity of humans. A baby hung back behind its mother, but the rest snuffled around in search of food. Samantha and Damon cowered at the door of their tent, eyes wild with fear.

"They won't hurt you," Kyle said as Nick joined them. The three grabbed sticks and began banging them together, calling "Ha, ha, ha," until the creatures began scattering and retreating. The mother stood her ground longer than the rest, then finally turned, nudged her baby, and they too disappeared into the brush.

"What the hell were those?" Kurt Carter asked, scratching his head as he sauntered over from the neighboring tent.

"Javelinas," Kyle said. "Not wild boars. Aren't even part of the pig family."

"They're peccaries," Tom Harding said. "Do your homework before you come on a trip like this. I did."

"Tom's right," Ben said. "They're relatively harmless unless you threaten their young."

"Well, they didn't look harmless to me!" Samantha said. "Do you think they'll come back?"

"Not likely," Kyle said. "But we'll keep watch for you."

"Like you were doing tonight?" she asked, her voice dripping with sarcasm.

"Off to bed, Ms. Manning," Ben said. "We've got you covered."

With a humph, she disappeared along with her husband.

"One night down, nine to go," Nick said. "You ready for me to take over?"

"I'll do it," Kyle said. "Ben was just waking me when the javelina panic occurred."

"Thanks. See you at three," Nick said.

*****

At sixes and sevens at home, Harriet decided to go into school. She had tried Kyle several times over the last few days, always reaching his voicemail. If she could just hear his voice, she felt that she could face each day. Her sister Lucy had called, begging her to come for a visit, but she declined. Harriet adored her oldest sister, but sometimes it was difficult to be around Lucy's perfect world. Perfect house, perfect husband, perfect kids, perfect job, perfect friends. The list went on and on. Even now with Lucy and Rob living apart, she seemed to have the perfect separation.

As she parked and headed to her classroom, she bumped into the school head, Pru Marsden. "Harriet, hello! Good to see you. How's your summer started?" Pru had been at the school for two years now, and Hampton Meeting was a different place under her strong, enlightened leadership. Six feet tall, she was slender and stylish. Her short brown hair was swept back, and she wore a beige linen suit, a bright multicolored scarf tied jauntily round her neck.

"Great. Just got back from a trip to Arizona with my mom."

"Must've been hot out there."

"Not really. Her friends...our friends live in a moist, temperate valley, so the temperature was warm but bearable. And everything's green all year long."

"That sounds too good to be true. An oasis?"

Yes, she thought sadly, *too good to be true about sums it up.* "It is a pretty incredible place."

"What brings you to campus?"

"Just wanted to grab a few things."

"Of course. Don't let me keep you. I'm off to a board meeting, but if you stop by the office, Betty can give you your class list. You've got a lively bunch this year."

"Thanks, Pru." She changed course and headed to the school office housed in a small clapboard-sided cottage in the center of campus. After chatting with Betty and getting a folder of materials, she walked across the green to the classroom building, scanning her class list. She had a good group. The school endeavored to make all class assignments by early summer so teachers could plan and then let go of school matters for a month or so.

Her classroom was at the south end of the building with windows on two sides. A wide open, sunny room, there was a small alcove for coats and students' cubbies and another alcove with a tiny office area for her. She stepped in, the air heavy and musty with all the windows closed. She threw open the two in her office, and a fresh, gentle breeze filled her lungs. This was her sanctuary, where she felt safe, confident, and at peace.

She had barely settled in when her cell phone buzzed. Her mother. "Hey, Mum," she said, leaning back, waving to the greenskeeper who trimmed bushes outside her window. "What's up?"

"Just checking in. Did you have a good visit with Hazel?"

"Yup. No matter what she told you, I'm fine. No issues, no self-flagellation."

"I'm not prying. Just checking in with my beloved daughter."

"I've tried to call him. Several times. His phone's off."

"I could phone Leonora?"

"Please don't, Mum. I still haven't sorted out my feelings, and I really don't want others involved."

"Okay. Would you like to have dinner over the weekend?"

"That would be fine. I'm going riding with Karen Saturday, and we were thinking of dinner after. How about Friday or Sunday?"

"Let's plan on Sunday night, then. Come down for a walk if you like."

"I'll call you. Listen Mum, I'm at school right now, and I want to get a few things done, so I'll say goodbye, okay?"

"Of course, honey. Take care."

She clicked off, feeling guilty at lying to her mother. She loved her more than anyone in the world, but there were moments when Helen's concern felt suffocating, almost as if they were back in the closet at Hill House, cowering in the dark.

Had it all been too good to be true? A dream? A vacation fling? *Why can't I talk to him? Where is he?* She realized she should have let her mother call the Morgans. At least then she would know.

CHAPTER 38

"Only four days left," Ben said as he, Kyle, and Nick made camp. The trip had been relatively smooth, with guests and guides falling into comfortable rhythms and routines. Tonight, Nick was in charge of dinner prep and the others were setting up the tents. Tom Harding usually helped with this, and tonight was no exception. As they worked side by side, Tom said, "How's your sister doin'?"

"You mean Ruthie?" Kyle asked, surprised by the question.

The actor nodded. "I had a serious crush on our last trip."

"Oh?"

"I wanted more, but she was stuck on her elusive cowboy. They together yet?"

"Yep. Married with a baby."

"Wow, time flies, doesn't it? Is she happy?"

Kyle nodded. "If it's any consolation, no man's ever stood a chance with Ruthie. She's been stuck on Harley since she was ten."

"Lucky guy."

"Yep."

"How 'bout you, cowboy? You got a sweetheart?"

Kyle laughed. It sounded as if Tom was assuming his cowboy persona for the upcoming film. "No…yes…maybe. She's back East."

"And he's no cowboy," Ben called from the opposite side of the tent.

"Could've fooled me. What do you do?"

"I'm resident vet out at the new thoroughbred farm. My horse is a recent acquisition by Valley Stables."

"No kidding. What's that all about?"

"It's a dream of our dad's and his college buddy Spark, and between them, they have the money to make it happen."

"Interesting. I'd love to see it."

"Come for a tour when we get back."

"They looking for investors?"

Kyle dropped the tent flap and stared at Harding. "Don't know. You'd have to ask them. Better get on with this." His father and Spark had worked hard to keep the farm a secret until they had all the horses, and he knew they were still bidding on a few. Tom was probably just making conversation, but he decided he'd said enough. As he moved to the next tent, Kat stomped over to demand that her tent be placed near Dickie's and "away from that mosquito bog."

Kyle turned to face her. The rash was fading now and the blisters mostly healed, but she'd need a lot of makeup for any close-up shots for at least a few weeks. "No worries, there aren't mosquitos this high up."

"Says you. I want it right there," she said, pointing to a flat spot a short distance from where they'd erected Dickie's distinctive lime-green pup tent.

"I'd suggest we go a little closer to the main circle."

"Right there," she said, then stomped off. She had been hanging on Samantha Manning's brother for days, but Dickie seemed indifferent to her attentions. In fact, he remained aloof from most of the party except his sister and brother-in-law. Fortunately, he was an expert rider and had been invaluable in helping the novices, especially Angie and Willa. Kat had become Kyle's special burden, and she felt free to order him about from dawn to dusk.

Later that night, the others in bed, Nick stood watch as the brothers headed down to the river to fill water jugs. A full moon lit their path as they headed down, taking the mule that carried the water with them. Jugs and water bottles filled and loaded, they sat on the rocks by the swift-moving Gila.

"You miss Maggie and the kids?" Kyle asked.

"Every minute. I'd say this is my last trip. No more. But who the hell's gonna run 'em? Harley's gone, Robbie's not a strong enough rider, and we can't send Parker out alone. Maybe once Jeb finishes school, we can twist his arm. What about some of the new guys at the farm? Are there any decent riders among them?"

"And what do you think Harley's reaction will be if you suggest takin' 'em for a week or ten days? Have you talked to Dad? Maybe you should be looking for one or two new wranglers."

"It's not the wrangling as much as the Morgan's Run shit. Harley was one thing 'cause he's one of us, but runnin' a trip without a Morgan at the helm? That's probably not gonna fly."

"Then what's the answer? This is a cash cow for the ranch, isn't it?"

"We could survive without it. I'm thinking one a year and we take turns. Robbie could do it with help. When Charlotte gets bigger, Ruthie could go. Hell, Beth could do it, and you, bro."

Kyle raised his hands. "No way I'm leading one of these. Lackey yes, but head honcho? No can do."

"I'm sure we'll figure it out. Maybe once Valley Stables is up and running, I can get Langdon back for one trip a year. Trouble is, then I'd have to go too," Ben said, grinning. "Half the fun is seein' him on the trail with these guys. He'd have thrown your girlfriend off a cliff two days ago."

"Kat is not my girlfriend. She considers me her manservant. She only has eyes for Dickie, even though he pretty much ignores her."

Ben laughed. "So seriously, what about your girl? What's goin' on with that?"

"As I told you, I'm giving her space."

"For what?"

"To figure out what she wants."

"She wants you, buddy. I've seen the way she looks at you."

"When I get back, we'll see. It's actually been good to get away from my phone so I wouldn't be tempted to dial her up."

"Mine's right here," his brother said, pulling his cell from his pocket. "Although reception's crap here. You can use it tomorrow when we climb the Notch."

"Thanks, but I'll wait it out."

"Suit yourself, my martyred brother."

"Ha-ha," he said as they started back with the mule.

CHAPTER 39

Harriet met Karen Childs at the family's stables at two. Her dearest friend since their teens, she hadn't seen her in over a month. "Hey, girl," Karen called from the far end of the barn. "Got our two beauties all saddled and ready."

The friends hugged and headed out into the sunlight. "Long time, no see," Karen said. "You look well. How was your trip?"

"Lots to tell," Harriet said, smiling at her friend. Short and compact, Karen had curly, reddish brown hair, stuffed under a faded baseball cap. Her blue eyes twinkled, and she had the ruddy cheeks of the farmer she was. Still single with a string of boyfriends in her past, she'd had several marriage proposals, but something was never quite right. Karen and her brother, Brick, managed the family stables.

"Great, let's go."

Effortlessly, they mounted the two stable-owned Arabians and trotted toward an open field. They headed for the eighteen-mile bridle path that circled the village and ran along either side of the peninsula. The first few miles took them along a ridge that overlooked the river on their right and, on their left, miles of farmland that gave way to stone-walled fields of wildflowers as they rode past Mavis LaSalle's property, a popular wedding destination. The property included Mavis's gracious home as well as a huge, refurbished barn and two additional buildings housing a spa and small inn. As they passed the entrance to the property and the sign for

Cove Inn and Spa, a red Mercedes convertible sped by, and the lady herself waved, a bright green scarf streaming out the window in her wake.

"How does she do that?" Harriet asked, waving to their mothers' friend and a fellow Darn Yarner.

"Lots and lots of practice and watching thousands of old Hollywood movies. That scarf's her latest affectation. I believe this is her Isadora Duncan phase. Color changes every day, but she's been tootling around town all week like that."

"She's something, isn't she?"

"That's one way to put it. Let's get to the Knoll, and we can stop and have a drink."

They rode awhile longer, ascending to the highest point on the peninsula, a grassy spot that overlooked the village. As they sat on a flat boulder the locals had dubbed Chair Rock, Harriet sighed. "My favorite place in the world."

"Mine too, but maybe tied with the top of the Nubble," Karen said.

"True!" she said, lifting her plastic cup and tapping Karen's. "This wine is nice."

"It's a new label from Cove Vineyard. So what's new with you? Tell me about the trip."

"It was good."

"Good? Can you possibly be more specific?"

"I met someone."

"I knew it! Tell me, tell me."

"He's a vet at his family's ranch. It's a big deal. They're raising racehorses."

"That sounds promising."

"Except that he lives three thousand miles away."

"That's just geography, sweetcakes. Love conquers all."

"Says the woman who's had a million boyfriends, been engaged fifty times, and never married!"

"That's me, babe, not you."

"That's what he calls me, babe."

"And you let him?"

"It's sweet the way he says it, not macho or chauvinistic."

"Oh boy, you got it bad. What're you doing back here?"

"Figuring things out."

"In a vacuum?"

"It's complicated. I saw Louis while I was out West. Or Arthur Greene, which is his real name."

Karen's jaw dropped. She'd been through the fall-out months after Louis, and she, like everyone else in Harriet's life, never mentioned his name. "Oh?"

"Yup, I can say his name. He has no hold on me anymore. He's nothing more than a bug I want to squish."

"How did that happen?"

"I'll tell you at dinner. Let's go. We've still gotta circle the village and head back."

"Stinker!" Karen said, hopping up on her horse.

The trail descended to an open pathway that ringed the village to the north, then turned south to the path that ran the length of the western shore past the marina, fishery, and research labs. Finally, they turned east again, and the horses broke into a gallop as they crossed the farm's grazing land. Wildflowers ran along the fences, and meadow larks and bobolinks flew from the tall grass as they passed.

Once in the barnyard, they slowed and finally slipped down. "Check for ticks," Karen said. "They've been ferocious this year. I can double check you too."

After picking a number of ticks from each other, they fed, groomed, and cooled down the horses. As Harriet put the brushes and grooming tools away, she said, "What do you think? Should I go home and change?"

"Don't bother. I'm not," Karen called. "Can we take your car?"

"Of course."

"Okay, let me get my purse. You've got a lot to tell, babe. And I want to hear gobs more about Mr. Gorgeous."

"How do you know he's gorgeous? I didn't say. He could have three heads and acne."

"Babe, you didn't see your moony face when you were talking about Mr. Hunky Vet."

"Oh Lord!" Harriet said as they strolled to her car. *Another Grand Inquisition!*

CHAPTER 40

Midday Sunday, the riders crossed the river and began the four-day journey back home. Miraculously, there hadn't been a complaint from Kat for two days. She was surer in the saddle and seemed to actually be enjoying herself. Angie and Willa were troupers, and they grew more comfortable every day. The others took care of themselves and seemed to be happy except for complaints about the food. They had packed fine wines and gourmet appetizers and foods, but they relied heavily on fish, caught by the guides, for most evening meals. Several of the riders were not fond of fish. Other foods had been brought to supplement, but palates were clearly wearing thin.

After they crossed the river, the trail climbed to Faulkner's Ridge, where they would ride the rest of the day and the next. Breathtaking scenery was their reward after the hard climb, and "oohs" and "aahs" sounded up and down the line. After a quiet night on the Ridge, they broke camp early the next morning. As the riders gathered the last of their belongings, Ben found his fellow leaders. "Hey, guys, just a heads-up. This is the worst stretch this morning. Thank God our campers are happy and strong. Have you ever been this way, Parker?"

Nick shook his head.

"And I haven't been this far out since we were kids," Kyle said. "I don't remember any of it."

"Well, it's tough on the horses and riders for about an hour. Lots of falling rock and narrow stretches. I'm wondering how we should handle it."

Nick pushed back his hat and said, "If you want my two cents, boss, I think we should send Dickie and Samantha on with the Carters, Tom, and Madeline. Then you can take Angie, I'll take Willa, and Kyle can bring up the rear with his girlfriend."

"Ha-ha," Kyle said, elbowing Nick. "But I agree. The only problem may be Madeline. She's not as comfortable as she'd have us think, and she's super sore and tired."

"Okay, then, I'll take Willa and Madeline, and Nick can take Angie."

"Sounds good," Nick said as they headed for the group to lay out the plan.

Dickie and the others set off first with admonitions to take it slow. As soon as they disappeared, Ben corralled his two. "Okay, ladies, Dandy and Annie are sure-footed and strong. They won't spook when the trail gets narrow unless you do."

"I don't see why I couldn't go with Tommy," Madeline whined. "He'd have taken care of me."

"It's just for a few hours," Ben said, hopping onto Rowdy. "Then you two will be reunited for the rest of the trip."

A pout on her face, she urged Annie forward, and Willa followed on Dandy.

"Geez, Louise," Nick said, watching them. "I don't envy your brother."

"He'll be fine. Willa's a great listener, and Annie's like a rock."

"Too bad we can't say the same for her rider. Ready, Angie?" Nick called as the dark-haired beauty took a sip of water.

"Truthfully, I'm scared to death," she said as Kyle helped her into the saddle.

Kyle patted the horse's flank, settling her down. "You're gonna do great. Keep Raine on a fairly tight rein, and she'll be fine. Remember, this stretch doesn't last long. The others are probably halfway through it already. Take care."

He turned to spy Kat attempting to mount Tara with not much luck. She was clearly tired and petrified. He paused, wondering if it would be better to walk the horses through, then realized that might be even more dangerous on the uneven ground. No telling where Kat might step with her silly designer boots. "Hey, hey, that's what I'm here for," he said, coming to her side.

"I can't…I can't do it. I want to go back. Please don't make me!"

"There really isn't another way. Come on, Kat, you can do this. I've been watching you. Your riding's improved, and you're ready." *Liar, liar, pants on fire.*

Kyle helped her up and gave Tara one more pat before mounting Blue. "I'll lead, so all you have to do is follow Blue's tail. Got it?"

Kat nodded, gripping the pommel and reins, her knuckles white, hands shaking.

They set off, the trail wide and solid for a half mile before narrowing. The ground was now rockier and the path little more than a foot wide in places. Blue did not appear concerned as he sallied forth slowly. Tara followed his lead.

"You doin' okay?" Kyle yelled.

"Hunky dory," she called. "How much longer?"

"'Bout a mile, maybe two. You can do it." Inwardly, he was cursing his fearless brother, who had plotted this course in collaboration with Damon Manning. Manning had insisted on rugged terrain and a loop rather than out and back. He also wanted to visit several cliff dwelling sites, which were hard to reach and only accessible to the adventurous. Two days earlier, they had camped at the base of a cliff, and Damon, Kurt, Dickie, and Tom had climbed up to the caves with Ben leading.

Around the next bend, Blue slipped, rocks cascading down the sheer face. "Geez," Kyle muttered, reining him tightly as the horse regained his footing.

That was it for Kat. She froze and refused to go another inch. There was no room to dismount, and he couldn't be sure that Blue wouldn't spook. "Listen to me, Kat. You're putting yourself and Tara in danger by stopping. I'm gonna take it slow, and I need you to follow. There's no other way. You can't go back. Tara'll be fine." He gritted his teeth, inwardly cursing his brother again as he urged Blue forward. "It's better up here. Just a little farther."

As he proceeded, he was relieved to hear Tara's soft nicker behind them. *Good girl,* he thought. *Keep going, don't look down.* The others had completely vanished, and he could no longer see Tabasco's enormous flank, leading Raine in his wake. Would that they all rode mustangs. Mustangs were the most sure-footed on this kind of terrain.

Around the next bend, he glanced over his shoulder. Kat held the reins tightly. *Good girl.* Then he looked up and saw she had her eyes shut tight. *Geez!* "Kat, open your eyes, for Christ sake! Tara needs you to guide her!"

"Okay," came a soft voice.

They continued slowly along the narrow trail for a mile or so. Then it widened slightly, and the ground became a little more compact. Kyle still couldn't see the others ahead, but he wasn't worried. He glimpsed firmer, wider trail ahead. The canyon shelf was not so sheer, and the hill downward was covered with brush. Above them, pebbles and rocks fell from time to time, but the horses stayed steady. *Thank the Lord*, he thought as the trail widened and Blue stepped more confidently.

There was a slight descent ahead, then, he hoped, more open space. "Almost there!" he called to Kat as Blue began descending. Kyle reached a small clearing along the Ridge and turned to spy Kat and Tara just making their descent. As he watched, he saw that she'd let go of the reins and was grasping the pommel in a death grip. "Geez, Kat, get ahold of the reins!" he called as Tara began to skid.

As Kyle watched in horror, rider and horse skidded to the ground and over the edge. He ran back in time to grab hold of Tara's lead. The horse's eyes were wild with fright, pleading with him. Kat was pinned under the horse, still holding the pommel, screaming.

Kyle lay flat on the ground and yelled, "Kat, shut up. You're scaring her! Stay completely still. Do you hear me?"

It appeared that a small ledge covered in brush had broken their fall. Below the ledge was a drop of several hundred feet. There was no way he could pull them up alone, and he wasn't sure that he and Blue were strong enough to do it. The horse lay on her side, still and panting. *Thank God it's Tara*, he thought. *Most horses would be wriggling their way to instant death*. His mind raced, wondering if he dared let go, but realized that for the moment, they were okay. For once, Kat had followed his instruction and lay still and quiet to the side of the horse, her right leg under Tara, tangled in the stirrups.

"Okay, girl," he said, patting Tara head. "We're gonna get you outta here. Promise."

He whistled and, to his surprise, Blue responded, trotting slowly back up the path. "Good boy," he said as the horse nuzzled his shoulder. "Okay, Kat, listen to me. We're gonna try and pull Tara up to stand. If we succeed, I want you to hold on to her for dear life. As she comes up, grab anything you can to stay connected to her. Do you understand?"

She nodded. "I think my leg's broken."

"Do you think you're strong enough to hold on?"

"Do I have a choice?"

"There's really no other way."

She nodded, eyes pleading.

Kyle stood, still holding Tara's lead, knowing that if she began to slip, there would be nothing he could do. He grabbed two coils of rope and considered their options. Fortunately, there was enough rope for a makeshift cradle. As he passed it down, Kat followed his instructions and looped it around Tara's flank. "That's great," he said, "now throw the loop back."

The rope dropped several times, but finally, he caught it. He then made a loop with the second coil and threw it to Kat, instructing her to tie it around her waist. When that was done, he studied the situation. Saving Kat was his top priority and he needed to stay focused on her, but he feared if Tara went over the cliff, she'd take Kat with her. Blue too. *This has to work, buddy, or we're all screwed.*

"Okay, Kat, you ready?"

"I'm scared."

"I know, but I'm not gonna let you fall. Trust me. I've got you, and Blue has Tara. If she starts to slip, start kicking your leg free as soon as she passes. I have you. Do you understand?"

Wide-eyed, she nodded as a tear streaked down her dusty cheek.

Kyle tied Tara's rope to Blue's pommel. "Okay, buddy, you gotta use everything you've got. You ready?" Clicking his tongue, he yelled, "Hee-yah!" and urged Blue forward. Tara began to move upward inch by inch. As she understood what was happening, the gentle horse began scuffling, attempting to gain a footing.

"Whoa, hold on girl. Not yet," he called, seeing Kat grimace with pain yet not making a sound. *Good girl*, he thought. As Blue faltered and lost ground, woman and horse began slipping back, closer to the edge. Kat grabbed futilely at the brush around them.

"Come on, boy," Kyle said, holding Kat's rope while inching up to take hold of Blue's bridle. The horse regained his footing for a few seconds, then paused, unsure what to do.

Kat cried, "I can't hold her. She's falling, and I can't get free!"

Kyle looked back to see Tara listing to one side. The rope was still tight round her but wouldn't stay there much longer if she continued sideways. "Come on, boy," he said, slapping Blue's flank. The horse lunged forward, but it was clear he wasn't strong enough. Tara's distress was mounting, and it wouldn't be long before she pulled herself free. Kyle took hold of both ropes and pulled along with Blue, but they still couldn't do it.

"What's wrong?" Kat called as Tara slipped further.

"Remember what I said," he called. "Start kicking to free yourself if she goes." He turned back, looping Tara's rope over his shoulder, and gave it everything he had. It was clear it would not be enough. As Tara's weight began to shift downward, he held tight to Kat's rope, closed his eyes, and prayed. Suddenly, everything stopped, and he looked up to find his brother and Nick beside him.

"Geez, bro, what's this all about?" Ben asked as both men took hold of Tara's line, urging Blue onward.

Between the three of them and Blue, Tara began to move slowly upward. As she reached level ground, she knelt, then stood. Kat clung to her side until Kyle could let go and grab her. Her foot was still stuck in the stirrup, ankle twisted.

"Okay, I got you," he said, pulling her free. She collapsed in his arms, sobbing. "Hey, you're okay now. You're safe. You were incredibly brave, Katherine Doolittle."

She raised her tear-streaked face to him. "You think so?"

Kyle smiled. "I know so."

CHAPTER 41

Kat's leg and ankle were broken. No cell phone service meant no way to get word to the ranch. "I've set them, but no way she can ride for two more days," Kyle said to his brother. "You're gonna have to leave us and send a chopper back when you get home."

"We could sling her over one of the horses and bring her out that way."

"Not for two days when there's an alternative. We'll be fine. Take Tara, and I'll keep Blue and ride back as soon as the chopper picks her up. I know the way from here. You'll get service before you get back, so I'll only be a short distance behind you."

"I can stay too," Dickie said.

Ben shook his head. "No, I need you. We've still got ten people to get back safely." He turned to Kyle. "You sure about this, bro?"

"Yup. Now get going. The sooner you can make a call, the sooner we can get the hell outta here."

"Why don't I stay with your guys?" Angie said. "I've had enough riding, and I can go to the hospital with Kat."

Ben shrugged. "Okay by me. Parker, let's get food and water unloaded for them."

As the three watched the party ride off, Kyle wondered, *What in the hell am I gonna do with these two in the middle of nowhere?*

*****

"I've called and called," Harriet said as Elise listened quietly. "I'm really at my wit's end. Why hasn't he at least acknowledged my calls? Even if he's washed his hands of me, doesn't that seem odd to you?"

"Have you checked with anyone else out there? Maybe he lost his phone."

"Mother wanted to call the ranch, but I told her not to."

"Because?"

"Because I didn't want to… I wanted to stay… Honestly, I don't know. It seemed like it would be admitting that I cared and was interested."

"And that's a bad thing because?"

"Because I'm scared," she said, breaking down, tears streaming down her face. "Of calling and speaking to a stranger. Scared that it was all a dream. A vacation fling for him. I'm scared to find out that he's moved on and blocked me from his life."

"Does that seem to ring true when you think of the man you know?"

"No, not at all, but what do I know? The only other man I allowed into my life robbed me blind and broke my heart."

"Does Kyle remind you of Louis?"

"Not in the slightest. Polar opposites, in fact."

"In what ways?"

"Louis was all about himself. Couldn't pass by a mirror without preening. Every romantic gesture was about how magnanimous *he* was, not how much he wanted to please me. Kyle is kind and generous because that's his nature. He does what he does out of what seems like genuine caring with no ulterior motive. He's one of the most selfless people I've ever met."

"So why would you assume that this relationship would progress the same as previous relationships?"

"Because all those things I just said? They are observations after knowing him for not much more than a week. He could be a selfish cad for all I know."

"Hmm, do you believe that?"

"No… Yes… I don't know, but why hasn't he called?"

"As I said, maybe he lost his phone."

"Elise, we've been seeing each other for what, eight years? I know I'm supposed to figure things out on my own, and we've made so much progress. I'm so grateful for that, but now, at this moment, I need *you* to tell me what to do."

The therapist smiled. "I think you know."

"But I need you to say it. Please."

Elise stared at her for a few seconds and then said, "Why don't we try this? You say what you think you should do, and I'll either nod or shake my head. That way, it's still your words."

"Okay, I do nothing."

Elise shook her head slightly.

"I call the ranch and try to reach him that way." Harriet watched as Elise broke into a grin. "I don't see a nod."

"Do you need one?"

"No, I'll call as soon as I get home. Thank you."

CHAPTER 42

"Hi, honey, wonderful to hear your voice," Leonora said. "How your mom?"

"She's great, thanks," Harriet replied, swallowing hard. "Leonora, I'm calling because I've been trying to reach Kyle."

"Oh, he didn't tell you? His brother roped him into going on a ten-day pack trip. They've been out eight days. The group's due back Wednesday. We've been a little worried 'cause we haven't heard from them, but there's little cell phone service out there. Kyle's the least tied to technology of any of our kids, so I'm willing to bet his phone is off and probably sitting up in his room. Want me to check?"

"Oh, no, that's okay."

"Ben has a phone, but as I say, service is spotty at best. Can I give him a message? Have him phone when he returns?"

"Thanks, Leonora, that would be great. I did leave him a voicemail too."

"Well then, I'm sure he'll be in touch when he returns, honey."

They rang off, and Leonora turned to find her husband standing over her, his expression grave. "What's wrong?" she asked.

"Ben just got called. There's been an accident."

"Oh, Benny!"

"Everyone's okay, but one of the guests has broken her leg. They need a helicopter. I'm gonna phone now."

"Why don't you try Spark first. Doesn't he keep one in Grenville? Probably be quicker."

"That's why I love you," he said, kissing the top of her head.

*****

After hanging up, Harriet went online and booked a ticket to Grenville. She then called and reserved a room at a B and B in town and also reserved a rental car. She packed a small bag, called her mother, who did not answer, then called the school office to alert them that she would be away. She tried Helen one more time, then left a voice message. *Easier this way*, she thought, locking the house and heading for the Providence airport.

She had booked a red-eye. As soon as she was buckled into her seat, she took magnesium pills, which always helped her sleep like a baby. Leaning back, she closed her eyes. *I'm taking action at last*, she thought, falling asleep before the plane reached cruising altitude.

*****

It was too late for Spark's helicopter to take off Monday night. Kyle and his companions ate a sparse dinner. Kat was in a lot of pain, and they made her as comfortable as they could. He had brought a small medical bag and they had a first aid kit, but aside from ibuprofen, there wasn't much to give her for the pain. "You go to sleep now," he said to Angie. "I'll stay up with her. Gotta keep watch anyhow."

"Why don't you wake me so you don't have to be up all night?" Angie asked.

He smiled. "Thanks, I'll be fine. Night."

They heard the chopper shortly after dawn. Despite his best efforts, Kyle had fallen asleep leaning against Kat's tent. He shook himself awake and stood, stretching. "Okay, ladies, your ride is here."

The helicopter landed, and Kyle was not surprised to see his father hop out. "Hey, son," he called, shielding his eyes from the sun.

Father and son hugged, and Kyle said, "Boy, am I glad to see you, Dad. Is this Spark's fancy helicopter?"

"You betcha. Much quicker than waitin' on the sheriff."

"Kat's the patient. Broken tibia and ankle. I've set 'em, but not sure what an orthopedist will say."

"Okay, guys, let's get her in," Ben Senior called as two men emerged with a stretcher.

"Angie's going with her, and I'll ride back on Blue."

"By yourself? I don't like it, son. It's been a long while since you've been out here."

"I'm fine. Ben's given me all the trail maps. It's less than a two-day ride."

"You sure?"

"Yup."

"Your girl's been callin' for you."

"Harriet?"

"Yup. Phoned and talked to your mother 'cause she couldn't reach you."

Kyle grinned. "All the more reason to get back to civilization."

"Wanta try and reach her now? We can probably get through."

"No, I'll wait, listen to her messages, then phone."

"Okay, then."

"Dad?"

"Yup?"

"If she calls again, tell her I'm okay."

"Will do. Take care, son."

"I'll clean up and start off in a few. Hey, ladies, good luck," he said as Kat was loaded into the back of the helicopter.

"Wait, stop!" she called, reaching out to him. "Thank you for saving my life, Kyle Morgan."

"You did good, Ms. Doolittle."

"If you weren't taken, I'd ask you to marry me right now."

He laughed. "When you get back to civilization, you'll come to your senses. Take care. If you guys are still around, I'll see you back at the ranch." He leaned over and gave her a hug.

Kat snuck in a chaste kiss as he pulled away. "Can't blame a girl for trying."

"Take care of her, Angie," Kyle said as the door shut, and he stepped away, waving to his dad.

"Now to find our way home," he said to Blue as he packed up the remains of camp. They'd taken the mules, so tent and food, or what little was left of it, went on Blue.

CHAPTER 43

Shortly after landing at Grenville, Harriet was in her rental car, headed for the Valley. Bleary-eyed, she checked into the Honeysuckle B and B at twelve thirty. She knew that the pack trip wasn't due in till the following day, so she decided a brief nap was in order. Midafternoon, she called Aria's cell and asked if she was free for dinner, which she was. They agreed to meet at the Bulldog at six thirty. She then came down to the lobby and found proprietor Lacey Cole at the desk. "Hey, honey, your room okay?"

"Very nice, thanks."

Lacey, a petite blonde with dark rimmed glasses, smiled. "We try. My husband, Dale, just went to get groceries. Is there anything you need? We have a fridge where you can keep food."

"I'm fine for now, thanks."

"How long are you stayin' in our beautiful valley?"

"At least till Friday. My return flight is open-ended, though."

"Ah-ha, I see. Well, the room is yours as long as you need it."

"Thanks, Lacey," she said, heading out. As she walked to her car, she met Dale Cole laden with bags. A tall, lanky man with an angular jaw and thick salt-and-pepper hair, cut short, he had a warm smile and kind blue eyes.

"Hey, I'm Dale."

"So glad to meet you."

"I'm guessing Lace has you all settled?"

"Perfectly. Thanks."

"Do you know Saguaro?"

"Yes, this is my second visit."

"Okay, then. We have a happy hour of sorts from five to seven, if you're interested. You're also welcome to join Lacey and me for dinner. I'm grilling trout."

"That is so kind of you, but I have plans."

"Well, if anything changes, give us a call, and we'll set another place."

Harriet waved, marveling as she had so many times at the Valley family. One felt its embrace wherever one went.

She drove the short distance to Morgan's Run and parked at the Big House. She knew she probably should have phoned ahead, but here she was. She knocked at the front door, and Leonora answered. "Why, honey, what a surprise! Did you tell us you were coming and I forgot?"

"No, I'm sorry. It was kind of a spontaneous decision. I hope I'm not intruding."

"Of course not. Come in. Where are you staying?"

"I've got a lovely room at the Honeysuckle in town."

"Nonsense. Look at all the rooms we have between here, Ben's, Beth's, and Ruthie's."

"I'm fine, really."

"Would you like something to drink? Of course you would. Come on back to the terrace, and Carmela will bring us something. Iced tea? Lemonade? Water? It's almost cocktail time. How 'bout a glass of wine?"

"Water would be fine. I'll only stay a few minutes."

Leonora disappeared into the kitchen, returning a minute later. "Come on out and sit. Carmela will bring a tray."

Settled with drinks on a lovely valley afternoon, her host turned to her. "I'm guessing you're here to see Kyle?"

"Yes. I understand they get back tomorrow?"

"The group, yes, Kyle, no. He may take a bit longer. There was an accident. One of the guests broke her leg. The rest of the group went on and left Kyle with her and a friend until this morning. The women were evacuated by helicopter. My husband's with them at Valley Hospital. He should be home soon."

"Is Kyle with him?"

"No, Kyle stayed back and is riding back alone."

"Oh?" Harriet's face fell.

"Not to worry, honey. He's an experienced rider, and he knows the trails. He'll be fine, but he may not reach us till Thursday. Depends on how hard he pushes."

Harriet nodded but said nothing.

"So you hopped on a plane and came back to us?" Leonora asked.

"I know, it sounds crazy. I'm not, but I left things so abruptly. I wanted to... to make things right, if that makes any sense."

"If it's not prying, what would right be?"

Harriet stared at her for a few seconds before replying. *I'm looking at mama bear, protective and ready to fight for her young.* "Honestly, I'm not sure. I know my mother told you a bit of my history."

"Yes."

"It all happened so quickly with Kyle, and I wasn't sure... The last thing I'd want to do is inflict my past and my neuroses on him. I was also so terribly hurt years ago that I've been reluctant to get close to anyone. Your son is an incredible man, and he deserves to be with someone who is whole and normal."

"And that's not you?" Leonora asked, a slight smile playing around the corners of her eyes.

"I don't know."

"Well, for what it's worth, I've learned that none of us are 'normal.' We all have our idiosyncrasies and issues. I know I do."

"You're kind to say that when I'm sure you'd rather have me three thousand miles away."

"Not true, and I'm not being kind, just realistic. Honey, my son knows his own mind, and he cares about you. That I know. What happens to you two from here on is your business, not mine."

They talked awhile longer, and Harriet handed a slip of paper to Leonora. "This is my cell."

"Stay and have supper with Ben and me."

"Thanks, but I'm eating in town tonight. I'll check in tomorrow. If there's any news, please let me know."

"You sure you won't change your mind and stay with us? I can phone Beth, Ruthie, or even Maggie. They'd be delighted to have you, as would Ben and me."

"Thanks, but you've done enough. I'm all settled in at the Honeysuckle."

Leonora nodded. "Lacey and Dale are wonderful hosts and dear friends. If you change your mind, just let me know."

*****

The trail was clear and marked by the passage of Ben and the others, and Kyle made good time. He rode until nearly sunset and camped on the Ridge just before the descent that would lead him back to the river trail and home. *Home and the chance to hear Harriet's voice.* He fell asleep smiling.

CHAPTER 44

"You could have knocked me over with a feather when I got your call," Aria said, hugging her outside the Bulldog. "What are you doing back here?"

"I think I made a huge mistake," Harriet said.

"About Morgan?"

"Let's go in and eat. I'm starved."

They both ordered Bulldog burgers, fries, and Desert Ambers on draft and went to a back booth.It was early, and there were a half-dozen patrons, all men. They watched the two gorgeous women's progress until they disappeared into the booth. "Ever wonder what a meat market feels like?" Aria asked, grinning.

"I think this is one of the few places on earth where men outnumber women," Harriet said as they sat.

"So? What's going on?" Aria asked. "I mean, I'm super glad to see you, just shocked."

"I love him."

"That much was obvious."

"And I can't turn my back on that until I see where it goes."

They spent the rest of the meal chatting about life, love, and Valley gossip. Harriet had very few friends besides Karen, and she really enjoyed Aria's company. Spark's chef had a quick wit and a great sense of humor, but most of all, she was a sensitive soul underneath the playgirl façade, and Harriet sensed a kindred spirit.

*****

Wednesday morning, Kyle woke in a driving rain storm, his clothes and bedroll soaked through. *Yet another reason to get home in a hurry*, he thought, since he'd sent the rest of his clothes on the mules. He packed up and quickly saddled Blue, who was restless with the rain and the rumbling of thunder in the distance. He fed the horse but wasn't hungry, so he grabbed a protein bar and stuffed it in his back pocket. They had gone about a half mile in what the locals called a monsoon rain, when they came around a bend to a horrifying sight. Twenty feet ahead, the entire trail was gone, washed out, nothing but sheer rock face for at least thirty yards.

"Shit," he muttered, reining Blue back. Fortunately, the trail was wide enough for them to turn around, but now what? He hadn't the faintest idea how to circumvent the slide, and with visibility about five feet, he decided to head back to where they'd camped for the night and find a modicum of shelter under the trees. Lightning streaked across the path ahead, but he had to push on. The danger of staying where they were was greater than the chance of a lightning strike. He prayed the storm would pass quickly. "Come on, boy," he urged, and Blue followed his lead, as eager as his rider to take shelter away from open ground.

They huddled in a small clearing to the side of the trail for several hours until the rain let up and finally ceased altogether. The sky cleared, and the day grew hot. This was desert, not Saguaro Valley, and the hot humid air was oppressive. He dug inside his pack and found Ben's maps. After studying them, he decided that their only choice was to go back over the Ridge and descend and take the river trail marked on the map. It was longer and less scenic, but it would eventually get him home. It was at least a day's ride to where they could make the descent, and they would need to pass the narrow stretch where Tara and Kat had fallen, but he couldn't see any other way.

"Okay, Blue, let's get a move on and pray there aren't more washouts ahead." No sooner had he spoken than they encountered a five-foot gap where the ground had sunk away. Before he had time to consider his next move, Blue took off and cleared the space easily.

"Good boy," he said, thankful for all Blue's years in the steeplechase world. If he'd ever needed a jumper, it had been now. Only a couple of the stable horses could have cleared the gap so easily.

On they went, slowly and carefully climbing, then descending. At nightfall, they found a small alcove to the side of the trail. "This'll have to do, boy," he said, pulling out the granola bar and feeding half to the horse and chewing the other himself. They had almost no food left, but plenty of water. As he fell asleep, Blue's lead in his hand, Kyle looked up, thankful for the clear starry sky. "No rain, please," he muttered before falling into a deep sleep.

CHAPTER 45

"Something's wrong," Ben said to his parents as they stood in the stable yard. "He should be back by now."

His father shook his head. "I'm gonna call the rangers, see if they have any information about conditions after all that rain."

"What will I tell Harriet?" Leonora said. "She's called several times."

"That we don't know anything yet," her husband said. "Our son knows how to survive out there."

"The hell he does," his son said. "I'm sorry, Dad. Kyle's a decent rider, but he knows shit about trail riding. After all his years back East, he's clueless. He's a vet, for Christ sake."

"That's enough," Ben Senior said. "I'm gonna phone the rangers, and then we can update Harriet. Maybe she'd like to come over to the house?"

"Yes, that's a good idea," Leonora said as Maggie and the kids drove in. "I'm going back with them."

"Okay, darlin'. I'll phone when I know something."

*****

It was after ten that night when the family gathered at the Big House. The children had been put to bed upstairs, and the adults sat in the living room. Ben,

Maggie, Beth, Lang, Robbie, Hope, Ruthie, and Harley sat with the elder Morgans along with Spark, Jeb, Amy, and Harriet.

Ben Senior gazed around the room, his expression grave. "According to the rangers, there've been washouts all along the Ridge. He's been cut off, no doubt about it. He'd have to switch back and get to lower ground, if he can. Then he can follow the river."

His son shook his head. "Which is what our whole group should have done. If we'd followed the goddamn river none of this would've happened."

"Or, if I'd gone with you as I should have in the first place," Harley said.

"I expect that guilt isn't gonna get us anywhere," Ben Senior said. "It's nobody's fault. Thing now is to figure out what to do and do it."

"Would the chopper help?" Spark asked. "I can have the guys standing by."

"Let's give 'em time to ride out," his friend said. "What do you guys think? If he had to go back till he could get to lower ground?"

"At least a day or more to get down, then another to get back."

"I vote that we send the helicopter up to see where he is," Leonora said. "That should put our minds at rest."

"'Cept it'll be damn near impossible to see him on most of the river trail. Too many trees and brush," Harley said.

Ben Senior said, "Let's do it anyway. Spark?"

"I'll have it ready at dawn."

"I'm coming with 'em," his friend said.

"Me too," Spark said. "More eyes, the better."

"Will you guys radio back?" Harley said. "Pepper will be rested enough by then. I'll ride out as soon as we know his location."

"Not without me, you won't," Ben said. "I got him into this mess."

"Do you think that's wise? You're exhausted, and your family hasn't seen you for ten days," Robbie said. "I can go with Harley. It's an easy ride along the river."

"I'll go," said Harriet quietly. "If there's a horse I can ride, I'd like to go."

Maggie nodded. "Then it's settled. Harley and Harriet will ride as soon as we hear word." She turned to her husband. "Robbie's right. We need you here."

CHAPTER 46

Midmorning, Spark called the Big House from the helicopter to say they had spotted Kyle and Blue on the river trail. Horse and rider had made it down from the Ridge and were making slow progress. With any luck, they'd reach the ranch by nightfall. Harriet met Harley at the ranch. Nick had Pepper and Royal saddled and ready to go. "Royal's a good ole boy," he said as she stared up at the large Morgan. "A little bit of spirit, but nothing you can't handle."

"He and Pepp get along fine," Harley said. "You ready?"

"As I'll ever be," she said. Nick helped her mount the tall horse. She wore jeans and a canvas jacket and a wide-brimmed hat she'd bought in town. *I look like I'm headed for the Australian outback,* she thought, *but at least I'll be warm and dry.*

Nick rubbed Royal's nose. "He's probably out of food. I put food and water in the bags. Good luck. See you tonight, I hope."

They rode out side by side across open fields till they reached the Gila. As they started along the river trail, Harley took the lead. She marveled at the ease of the tall, wiry wrangler as horse and rider moved as one. *A centaur with a Stetson,* she mused, smiling at the image.

"You okay back there?" he called.

"Fine," she called back, the full weight of what she was doing suddenly sinking in. *What if he doesn't want to see me? Is this a colossal mistake?* Then she stuck out her chin and decided, *I'm going to make sure he's okay. Period. There's nothing wrong with that!*

*****

Kyle was exhausted. He'd barely slept the night before, and he was pretty sure he had a fever. *Just what I need, to die of some stupid bug after all the rest,* he thought, pushing onward, grasping Blue's mane to steady himself. He hoped he'd be able to remain in the saddle. There was no food, but plenty of water. Several times, he stopped to let Blue drink and splashed water on his own burning forehead. The first aid kit had three aspirin left, and he took them all, then hauled himself back onto Blue. "Good boy. Sorry I'm such a drag."

As the sun sank lower, he squinted through blurry eyes, the fever untouched by the aspirin. He couldn't tell, but it seemed as if he was nearing home. As he slumped forward, clinging to Blue, he saw figures approaching through the haze. *I must be hallucinating,* he thought as he collapsed, arms on either side of the horse's neck.

"It's him!" he heard through the fog. It sounded like Harley's voice. *Maybe I've gone off course and I'm coming to Valley Stables?* were his last thoughts before he began to slip off Blue toward the ground.

"Okay, buddy, we got you. You're gonna be okay," came through the haze, and Kyle looked up to see two faces staring at him. He blinked, not believing what he was seeing. Yes, it was his boss he'd heard, but crouching beside Harley was the woman of his dreams. The person he loved most in the world. The person he knew he could not live another day without, and she was holding him, kissing him, his cheeks, forehead, lips.

"Oh, Kyle, you're okay! I had to see if you were okay, and you are okay, my love, my sweet love."

Harley watched the tender reunion for several minutes before saying, "Okay, kids, we've gotta get movin' before dark. Morgan, you're with me. Harriet, I need your help for this one."

Together, they wrestled him up onto Pepper, then Harley hopped up behind him on the tall, strong Appaloosa. The horse seemed to take the extra weight in his stride, and as soon as Harriet mounted Royal, they took off, Harriet holding Blue's lead. Kyle drank some water but refused the offer of food. The elder Morgans and the entire family were waiting at the stables when they rode in shortly after dark. After hugs and welcome-homes, Kyle was bundled off to the Big House and put to bed. Harriet stayed with him until he fell asleep, then said good night to Ben and Leonora and drove back to town. They pleaded with her to stay the night, but she declined. "I'll be back in the morning," she said. "If that's okay?"

"Not only is it okay," Ben Senior said, "but we'd be mighty disappointed not to see you. Night, darlin'," he said, hugging her.

CHAPTER 47

"He's still asleep, honey," Leonora Morgan said as she opened the door the next morning around nine. "I hate to wake him."

"Of course not," Harriet said. "I'll come back later. I brought some muffins from the bakery."

"How sweet of you. Won't you come in and have coffee?"

"Thanks, but I've got errands to run in town. Can I do anything for you?"

"Thank you, sweetheart, but we're all set. Ben's gone with Spark up to the new farm, but Carmela and I are planning menus. We'd be glad to take a break and have coffee with you."

"Thanks, but I'll stop back later," she said. "Tell him I was by."

"Of course I will. See you soon, darlin'."

As Harriet drove away, Kyle came to the top of the stairs. "Mother, who was that?"

"Oh, you're up honey. Can Carm and I bring you some breakfast?"

"I'm perfectly capable of coming down and getting my own breakfast," he said, a tad too grumpily. "Now who was just here?"

"Harriet, sweetie. She said she's got errands to run, and she'll stop by later."

In less than ten minutes, he was showered, dressed, and downstairs. Carmela had left eggs and bacon in a warmer on the sideboard, and Harriet's muffins were now in a basket beside the warmer. He grabbed a plate, piled it with food, and sat at the table alone, thinking. As he ate his last bites, his mother appeared. "Oh, honey, I'm sorry. We were out picking strawberries. I hate for you to eat alone. I would have sat with you."

I've got to get my own place, he thought, smiling at her. "No worries, just grabbed a quick bite. I'm heading up to work in a bit."

"What? No one expects you to work today, darlin'."

"I'm fine. The fever's gone, and I'm sure as hell not lyin' around in bed all day."

"But…but Harriet said she was coming back."

"I'll call her. Maybe we can meet for a drink after work. Gotta run." He kissed her on the forehead, ran up to brush his teeth, and was out the door before she could say another word.

He had no intention of going to work, at least not for a while, but he called Patty to see how things were going. "Quiet so far, but all the inoculations should be in today, so tomorrow we can get that started."

"I'll be in bright and early, then. Maybe not today, though."

"I was going to call you 'cause Harley thought maybe you wouldn't be back till Monday. I was gonna ask how you wanted to proceed."

"Well, Harley's not my mother, and I'm fine. After being away, I've got some things I need to take care of today, but I'll be in tomorrow and over the weekend. Thanks for taking over while I was away."

"Honestly, there's not been a lot to do. I've been meeting Ned at Morgan's Run each morning to check on Misty. She's doing great, by the way, and I'm in love with Ned."

"He's a great guy. You telling me he's a cradle robber?"

"No, I just mean I love him as a friend. I had no idea that he was such a legend around here."

"That he is. Best wrangler the Valley's ever produced. Okay, then. Call if you need me, and I'll see you in the morning."

As he parked the truck, he was pleased to see the "Open" sign in the window of the shop. Forty-five minutes later, he emerged, small packet in hand, grinning.

It was just after noon when he parked in front of the Honeysuckle. When he stepped into the lobby, Lacey Cole greeted him with a huge basket of wildflowers in her arms. "Well, well, well, if it isn't the adventurer back from the wild. We heard about your ordeal."

"Front page of the paper?"

"No, I bumped into Spark's chef at the café this morning. She's a pistol, isn't she?"

"That's one way of putting it."

"What can I do for you, darlin'? You look as if you're about to bust a gasket."

"Is Harriet in?"

"Oh, so you know our lodger. Hmm… Now things are making sense."

"Lacey?"

"Top of the stairs, second door on the left, number three."

Kyle took the stairs two at a time and knocked softly.

Harriet had been reading and dozed off. When she opened the door still fuzzy from sleep, her eyes widened. "Kyle? What are you doing here? Shouldn't you be in bed?"

"To see you. And no, I'm fine. No need to lie around all day. I came to ask a pretty lady if she'd take a walk with me."

"Give me a minute?"

"Want me to wait downstairs?"

"No, of course not. Come in, I'll be quick."

She shut the door and went to the bathroom, brushing her teeth, combing her hair, and attempting to pull herself together. Her heart was pounding, and she was having trouble catching her breath. Finally, she opened the door and spied him.

At the window peering out, he turned and smiled. "Ready?"

CHAPTER 48

As they strolled down the street, he asked, "Have you eaten lunch?"

"No." Every fiber of her being tingled at his nearness. *This is what you've been waiting for all week. Why can't I find the words?*

He grinned. "Me neither. We could go to Gracie's or maybe grab something cool to drink from the café? Or ice cream?"

As they passed the café, she said, "Lemonade would be perfect."

"Comin' right up." He went to the take-out window and ordered two medium lemonades. When he returned, he said, "Wanta chance a walk behind the hardware store again?"

"Really?"

"Okay, lemme think. How about we take a short drive? My truck's at the Honeysuckle."

"Okay," she said softly.

He drove a short distance to a small lot for hikers. The trailheads for the river path ran north and south. "Here we are. Not that I want to relive my time along the Gila, but we can go south. There's a small clearing a short distance down. Come on," he said, taking her hand.

Harriet's knees wobbled as his touch undid her. She had never wanted a man more than she wanted Kyle Morgan. Five minutes later, they reached a shady glade with several benches scattered around. It was deserted, the only sounds the rushing waters of the river and wind in the trees.

As they sat, she set down her lemonade and turned to him. "Kyle, I want to explain… I mean I want to tell you why I'm here. I know it must seem crazy to you."

"Not a bit. You can explain all you want."

"I got home and realized what a fool I'd been," she said, taking both his hands in hers. "I love you, and I ran away because I was scared. Scared of being hurt. Scared of losing myself. Scared of intimacy. Who knows? Then there's our age difference. I worry that I'm too old for you. I could go on and on. It's all those things and many more. But it took me about thirty seconds at home…well, maybe a day, to realize that whatever happens with you and me, I needed to tell you how I feel and to see things through. I missed you so much, my heart ached. I had to see you, to tell you I love you, even if you don't feel the same. I'm not trying to pressure you. I just needed to tell the truth for me. I want to live my life honestly."

Kyle sat quietly listening, his fingers caressing her hands as she spoke. When she stopped, he said, "Is there more?"

She laughed. "No, I think that's it for now. That's a lot for me."

"I know it is, babe. Can I say something?"

"Of course."

"I was gonna say this anyway, but your words give me a hell of a lot more hope."

"About?"

He slipped from the bench to one knee and reached inside his pocket, bringing out the small box he'd carried for the last several hours. "Harriet Winthrop, I am in love with you so much so that I cannot imagine another day, another hour, another minute when you're not in my life. Your age is one of my favorite things about you, my darling. You are the only woman I want to spend the rest of my life with. I know this is rushing things," he said as he opened the tiny red velvet box, "and I fully expect you to say no, but I wanted to ask you if you would marry me. Don't feel like you have to answer now, today, this week or month. Please just think about—"

"Yes!" she said, hands folded in her lap now, tears streaming down her cheeks. "Yes, I'll marry you. Today, this week, next month, whenever you say."

His handsome face registered genuine shock. "You will?"

"Yes!"

"You don't want to think about it?"

"No," she said, reaching down to caress his cheek. "Not for one second. And I'm not crazy, promise."

"Oh, babe," he said, reaching out to her. "You might be crazy sayin' yes to the likes of me."

Harriet leapt into his arms, and they fell back onto the grass, wrapped in each other's arms. Their lips found one another for a deep, lingering kiss. Harriet felt him grow hard against her belly. "That's what I've been missing," she said, pulling back from the kiss to give him a mischievous smile.

"Only that?" he asked, kissing her slender neck, lips moving to the vee neck of her jersey, which revealed a tantalizing hint of cleavage.

"That's only the beginning, cowboy."

"So now I'm a cowboy?"

"After your recent ordeal, I should say you've earned the sexy cowboy award for Saguaro Valley and beyond," she said, rubbing her body against him, his cock growing harder, straining at his jeans.

"You know this is a public bridle path, don't you?" he asked as he cupped her breasts, teasing her nipples until they stood at attention.

"You chicken, cowboy?" she asked, her hand now stroking him.

"What do you think, babe?" He unzipped her jeans, pulling them and her panties off in the blink of an eye.

"I've missed you so much, my love. You have no idea," she said as she unbuttoned his jeans and released him.

"Yes, I do, 'cause I've missed you more." He grabbed a condom from his pocket, unwrapping it with his teeth.

"Here, let me do it." She slowly fit it over his cock, stroking, caressing, teasing as she marveled at his size that fit her so perfectly.

"Oh babe I love you and this." He grasped her naked buttocks, drawing her closer.

"That's what I'm counting on. I love you, fiancé, more than I could ever say. Please don't wait another second."

He smiled, gazing down at her as he slipped his fingers between her legs, finding her wet and ready for him. "How did I get so lucky? I love every inch of you. Let me show you how much."

He plunged into her warm depths, rolling them onto their side so they could gaze into each other's eyes every second of their lovemaking. His hands gripped her ass as Harriet's arms circled his neck. As they moved in luscious tandem, neither looked away, but kept the other's gaze, speaking their love wordlessly as their bodies surged to an explosive, almost blinding climax. They watched each other as their orgasm passed and their faces relaxed, eyes locked in calm, peaceful recognition of the other's love. Finally, he kissed her nose. "My sweet, beautiful babe."

"Can we stay here forever?"

"If it's okay with you that the party of riders spies us like this. I can hear 'em coming."

Her eyes grew wide. "Oh!"

"They're a half mile off," he said. "You learn to read the vibrations. Come on."

They dressed quickly and were sitting holding hands when five riders passed by, nodding. "Afternoon, folks!" Kyle called, grinning broadly.

When they disappeared, she turned to him. "Afternoon, folks? How can you be so casual after...after?"

"After I just made love to my future wife? 'Afternoon, folks' is my way of expressing how deliriously happy I am, babe."

Harriet leaned her head against his shoulder. "Me too."

"I am a little offended, though."

"Oh, why?" She turned to stare at him.

"Don't you even want to see the ring?"

"I caught a glimpse of it before. It looked beautiful."

"Not as beautiful as you, but here, my love." He opened the box to reveal an emerald surrounded by tiny diamonds in an antique setting. "I know emerald is your birthstone, but if you don't like it, we can go to Valley Jewelers or anywhere and find the ring you want."

"It's perfect," she said, holding out her hand.

Kyle slipped the ring on, and it fit perfectly. "You sure? I want you to have what you really want."

"What I really want is sitting right beside me. I love you, Kyle Morgan, *and* I love this beautiful ring."

"Oh babe he said, leaning over to capture her lips again.

Epilogue

The news of their engagement precipitated a hastily arranged dinner party at the Big House three days later. Helen flew in, as did Sam and Rose from Maryland and Buck Foster from California. Carmela and Aria collaborated on the glorious meal set out on the terrace, three tables festooned with colorful pottery and linens and buffet tables groaning with food. Toasts began as they sipped champagne and enjoyed Carmela's creamy flans and Aria's lace cookies. As the children played on the grass, Ben Senior rose, Leonora beside him, his arm around her shoulders.

"Well, folks, we've done it again! What a meal from the Southwest's two premier chefs enjoyed by the whole clan, including the Foster crowd. Jeb, too bad Mom and Dad couldn't come, but we'll get 'em to the wedding along with Harriet's sisters and friends. For now, let me say that my Nora and I couldn't be more pleased at the prospect of another daughter. How did we get so lucky with our Maggie, Rose, Hope, and now Harriet? And we thought our Bethie and Ruthie were it! Harriet, darlin', welcome to our family," he said, tipping his glass to her. "I can honestly say I've—we've—never seen our youngest son this happy, and it's all because of you. To Harriet and Kyle and a long and happy life together."

The toasts went on, some raucous, some sweet, some simple, some rambling. After ten minutes, Maggie felt compelled to give his brother Ben the hook. He grinned but acquiesced after "one more story." Finally, Kyle stood and took Harriet's hand. She stayed seated but gazed up at him as he spoke. "To my bride-to-be,

I can only say thank you for saying yes. You have made me happier than I ever thought possible. And to my family. Thank you beyond words, all of you, for giving me the amazing examples and role models of genuine, deep, loving, committed relationships. It's a lot to live up to, but I'm sure gonna try. I love you all very much."

As everyone clapped, Kyle raised his hands. "I have one more announcement. You know I love the Valley and you all, but this lady at my side has a life on the other side of the country that she's committed to, at least for the foreseeable future. I do not want to be separated from her for more than a day, so I've spoken to Dad and Spark, and they've agreed to ask Patty to take over as resident vet at Valley Stables. She's been doin' the heavy lifting for weeks anyway, and I know I leave the clinic in capable hands. I understand that there's no vet in Horseshoe Crab Cove, so I may throw my hat in the ring there. If not, I'll find something. Harriet and I leave in two days, and I'll look around then. So that's it, I guess. Like Sam and Rose, Harriet and I will be East Coasters, at least for the next few years."

Another round of applause.

Kyle was about to sit down, when he popped back up, hands held high. "Oops, one more announcement and then I promise to shut up. Harriet and I have discussed it, and we've spoken to Mom and Dad. They've agreed to host the wedding here at the ranch sometime this winter. Exact date to be announced."

With deafening applause this time, Kyle sat and kissed Harriet. As they broke apart and smiled at the family, she whispered, "Great job, cowboy."

Please read on for sample pages of **Song of the Spirit***, a fast-paced, breathtaking tale of courage and romance.* **Song of the Spirit***'s unforgettable characters intersect with historical events of the day, including the devastation of the Wounded Knee massacre.*

In the late 1800s, post-Civil War, two young Cheyenne sisters are wrenched from a loving family, kidnapped, and incarcerated at Rose Academy, a harsh Indian boarding school established to assimilate young Native people, teach them English, and eradicate their knowledge of traditional ways, considered inferior to the ways of the Washita (whites).

Forbidden to speak their native language, the sisters are whipped and punished; however, the school's harsh life fails to break their spirit. The eldest, Wind Flower, on the cusp of womanhood, excels academically, while continually planning their escape. Time and again, she runs away and is hunted down and returned to Rose Academy. There, she watches her beloved little sister's alarming transformation into a proper Washita girl. At the same time, Wind Flower finds love with a young Sioux renamed Caleb Green by his captors. Will these three courageous young people find freedom, or lose themselves and their way of life to the relentless cruelty of the Washita world?

Song of the Spirt
Chapter 1

Winnowing fingers of sunlight danced above them as the pair made their way through the forest. They'd been well taught by their elders to move like shadows in deep woods of silence. As they walked, scanning the ground, the older girl kept a watchful eye on her companion, never straying more than a few yards from her. It was the first year they'd been allowed to forage apart from the others, and she recognized this freedom was also a test of her responsibility.

Suddenly, the little one stopped, bending over to thrust her sharp wooden tool into the earth, grunting as she struggled with the task. Immediately, the older girl moved to her side. "Take care, little Dove. The roots are delicate, and Na'go needs them whole. Don't cut too sharply with your dibble, or there'll be nothing left of them."

She spoke softly, sensing that the child would greet her words with anger, yet unable to stop herself. The roots of the red turnip—much scarcer than its white cousin and a favorite of their people—were too precious to end up in shreds. Harvested intact, the roots could be used as the base of a delicious soup—perfect for the feasting in four days. In shreds, the roots wouldn't last the night before rotting.

As the older girl watched, her sister's chubby hands worried at the root, alternately pulling and chopping at it. Her face was all determination as she mined the tiny patch of tubers. "Go away, Wind Flower! I know how to do it. Na'go showed me!" she sputtered, her face the color of the root.

"I know, little one. I just—"

"And don't call me little one—my name is Laughing Dove!" she said chin thrust out, eyes blazing up at her sister. "I'm not little. I'm not! Father says I'll be much taller than you when I'm grown."

Recognizing the futility of further conversation, Wind Flower wandered off a little, hoping, albeit belatedly, to give her sister an unspoken message of trust. Glancing back, she saw Laughing Dove's shoulders relax. She smiled, full of love for the seven-year-old—the only one of her siblings still alive. These days, life for the Cheyenne was full of sorrow, but out in the woods, away from the reservation and the soldiers' prying eyes, Wind Flower felt happy and free. Free as her people must have felt years ago. Before the coming of the Washita.

The soldiers had permitted this gathering for the renewal of arrows and had not followed or pried into the sacred rite. They were busy elsewhere. Fighting still raged on the Plains, and the army had little time for the ragged band of Cheyenne and Arapaho they had corralled onto the reservation. It was the year 1887 by the white man's reckoning, and Wind Flower was thirteen.

Before her birth, there had been Sand Creek, the massacre by the evil White Hair's army. The old ones still spoke of Black Kettle and White Hair, who was killed at Greasy Grass. Wind Flower, two at the time of Greasy Grass, had often listened to whispered words of the battle the Washita called Little Big Horn. Whispered words of the man Custer and his defeat, hushed remembrances of a life that had all but vanished for the Cheyenne. The reservation on the Tongue River was the only home Wind Flower remembered. Still, she longed for the past her parents spoke of now in sorrowful whispers, late at night while their children slept.

When Wind Flower was small, Little Wolf had led the people to the Tongue River. Since then, the tribe had lived peaceably with their white jailers, but stories drifted back from the Plains where the Sioux fought on.

Of the journey to Tongue River, Wind Flower remembered little save for the intense cold and the wailing that seemed to envelop the tribe, blanketing them in sorrow and grief. The Great Spirit took her two brothers before the march began, and another sister, Pale Deer, died during the winter spent in the frozen caves of Lost Chokeberry Creek.

Over the years, Wind Flower had heard many stories of the events that led the Cheyenne to the land of the Tongue. Stories of the surrender at Fort Robinson with Crazy Horse and many of his Oglala Sioux with them. Stories of the Washita's betrayal and breaking of the treaty agreement, a betrayal that sent them to live in sickness and squalor with their Southern Cheyenne brothers. Stories telling of the fevers, chills, and aching of the bones that had taken her brothers and many more until Little Wolf dared to break away and push northward. Now, they lived under the white man's thumb, caged like animals but in relative peace, with less sickness and death than there'd been in the South.

"Someday," said Na'go, her mother. "Someday, we may be able to wrench the fire water from the hands of our warriors and their strength will return. Then we can break away to live in freedom once more." Na'go sighed when she spoke, knowing the elusive nature of freedom now that the Washita were here to stay.

Finding another patch of turnip, not the sweet red turnip but its more plentiful cousin, Wind Flower stooped and sank her dibble into the surrounding earth, teasing out the large white roots. She worked the smooth wooden spade carefully, shaking the dirt from the unblemished roots as she tucked them into her bag before moving on. Thus they continued until the sun reached its uppermost point. It was Laughing Dove who began complaining.

Dove, so like their mother with her dark eyes, long braids, and chubby figure, had trudged along behind her older sister, puffing noisily as the sun grew hotter, but now she'd reached her limit. There was no help for it. They would have to stop and rest, at least for a little while.

"Flower, I can't walk anymore," she whimpered, her voice echoing through the silence of the forest. The others were out of sight and hearing. To Dove, the woods, so cool and welcoming when they'd started out, now seemed full of unseen terrors.

Laughing Dove was afraid of everything, even the Wise Ones. Her sister knew she would soon be crying, imagining wild beasts all around them. "All right, my sister, we'll stop here and rest, but only for a little while." They'd reached a clearing, and Wind Flower set down her bag on the soft moss at the edge of the path, beckoning to her sister. "Come sit beside me, and I'll sing."

As an infant, Laughing Dove had napped little and cried incessantly, no matter who held and coddled her. She would drink quietly at her mother's breast, but the rest of the time, she howled. One day when her na'go was too busy to hold her, she was handed to her older sister.

Wind Flower took the tiny squalling baby and walked to the edge of camp, singing and rocking her. Round and plump even then, Laughing Dove's chubby, soft arms and tiny hands poked out of the blanket, reaching up to her sister's braids. Wind Flower continued singing and rocking, and before long, the baby quieted. The perpetual crying had ceased as Laughing Dove lay gazing adoringly at her sister.

Wind Flower's singing had always been a source of cruel teasing among her people. While the other women's voices reached to the skies, her voice sank to the earth, like a stone dropping from a high cliff. Before that morning, Na'go would motion for silence whenever her eldest daughter burst into song, but never again. As long as she held her tiny sister, Wind Flower was never silenced.

To this day, Laughing Dove could always be comforted by her sister's songs, and Wind Flower's kindred were forever grateful. A croaking girl's songs were always preferable to the screams of an unhappy child. Wind Flower felt needed. Upon her little sister, she could pour all the love she felt, all the love that her kindred had no time for anymore. As their world disappeared, wrenched away by the avarice of the Washita, her parents and elders had closed their hearts. Survival consumed every waking moment; there was no time for love.

Now the warm sunlight filtering down through the trees and her sister's singing lulled Laughing Dove to sleep. As her sister's breathing became regular, Wind Flower leaned down to kiss her cheek, brushing damp curls from her face. Perhaps Dove should have stayed behind, she mused, thinking of the long walk ahead of them. Back to the camp with over two hundred tipis arched in a huge crescent, curving toward the mountains beyond the plain. "Sleep, my little one," she whispered. "You'll need it."

Wind Flower leaned back, intending only to rest her eyes, but unexpected weariness overtook her. Before she knew it, she too was asleep—a deep, dangerous sleep full of dreams and remembrances. A sleep so deep that she failed to hear the horses. By the time the white man's voice broke into her dreams, it was too late. Too late to run, too late to hide.

CHAPTER 2

Wind Flower found herself in a familiar dream. Lost in the woods, she spied Ni'hu, her father, through the trees, calling, beckoning for her. Running to him, she cried, begging him to hold her. As strong, gentle arms enfolded her, Ni'hu whispered, "Be still, my daughter—you're safe." Suddenly, a shadowy figure stepped into the clearing—a Washita, his blue eyes blazing into hers. "Come, daughter." The Washita's eyes beseeched her to follow. They were her own eyes gazing back at her. Ni'hu held tight, and she was safe, but the Washita stayed too, close by, watching, waiting.

Suddenly, Corn Woman's face replaced that of the Washita. Corn Woman, tall and proud with her long, black braids tinged with gray. It was Corn Woman and her troubles that had brought the people together for the Renewal of the Sacred Arrows. Her shame had to be healed, and her brother, Bear Claw, had pledged the arrow renewal to bring the tribe back into favor—his sister's disgrace had touched them all.

Corn Woman struck Small Willow, her daughter, and soon after, the young girl killed herself in shame. For this, Corn Woman had been banished from the tribe forever. But her leaving was not enough—bad luck hung over the tribe like a black cloud, smothering what little good fortune remained.

The Cheyenne had suffered too much misfortune, and now Bear Claw hoped to bring back the luck. The ceremony, coming as it did at the height of the hunting season, promised prosperity and hope for all. The Sweet Medicine Chief would guide the Cheyenne on their journey, his powerful wisdom and knowledge delivering them out of the darkness.

Once the ceremony began, all the women and children would be confined to the tipis for four days and nights. Wind Flower recognized the importance of the arrow renewal, but she dreaded the confinement. Today, the air had smelled especially sweet. In her dream, she breathed deeply, gulping up the sweet crisp air, hoping to hold on to a little to take with her into the dark stuffy tipi. As she breathed in, half-asleep, half-awake, the air suddenly changed, growing thicker, and she began to choke.

"Hey, Cooky. What we got here? A couple of little squaws! Musta wandered off the reservation!" He'd already grabbed Laughing Dove. She screamed, struggling to free herself as the horses pawed the ground, circling them. Choking dust surrounded Wind Flower as she struggled to her feet. The man kept one arm around Laughing Dove's waist while he fought off the kicks and scratches of her older sister.

"Jesus, Cooky! Git off yer horse and help me. We got a regular wildcat here!"

Jumping from his horse, Cooky grabbed Wind Flower's arm and pulled her away. "Well, now, little missy. Ain't no call to carry on like that! We ain't gonna hurt ya. Gonna help, don't ya know? You'll be a dern sight better off where we's headed than you are now, I reckon. Now settle down, you hear?" His breath reeked of tobacco and whiskey, and his rough beard brushed against her cheek as he held her against him.

Laughing Dove called out, her wails echoing through the forest. Wind Flower kicked and scratched, desperately trying to free herself. "Ouch! Christ Almighty, Les—the little hellcat bit me!" He raised his hand, then brought it down full force, knocking her to the ground.

Sometime later, Wind Flower woke to the jostling of the horse and a sharp, stabbing pain in the small of her back from the saddle horn pressed up against her. They rode in silence on a well-worn trail across open ground. The land was unfamiliar to Wind Flower. She attempted to sit up but was pushed down roughly with a "Not so fast, my little bobcat. After yer clawing, you kin suffer fer a bit."

Twisting her neck, she vainly tried to catch a glimpse of her sister, but the other man rode alongside Cooky, and she was unable to see over or around the horse. No sound came from the other riders save for the clopping of hooves on the hard, dusty ground of the trail. Closing her eyes, she beseeched the Wise Ones Above to help them.

As it grew dark, the men began searching for a place to camp for the night. "We'll never make the train tonight, Cooky. Better to sleep here and make an early start."

At his words, Wind Flower woke with a start, her head fuzzy and sore. Cooky dragged her down, then shoved her toward the others. Finally, she spied her sister and discovered the reason for her silence. Laughing Dove had been gagged with the man's grimy bandana, now soaked with her tears. Wind Flower tried to go to her, but Cooky yanked her back. "Oh no you don't. Get us some wood, and hurry up."

When she pretended not to understand, he grabbed a fistful of twigs, gesturing. "Wood, you stupid squaw. Wood. And hurry up, or your sister gets it," he added, pointing a hunting knife at Laughing Dove, who cowered on the ground, eyes wild with fear. Wind Flower's gaze reached out to the frightened child, reassuring her before she turned to hurry off for wood.

Wind Flower understood the men perfectly, but Laughing Dove knew not a word of English, and with every word, her fear escalated. Her older sister decided to feign ignorance as well, perhaps learning more of their plans if they thought she didn't understand their talk. Jack Wilkins, a scout who had lived with the tribe for a time, had taught Wind Flower the white man's tongue. Jack, or Fire Hair, as the Cheyenne called the tall, gentle man with the head of flaming red hair, had lived for several moons in Lone Turtle's tipi, but then he had been called away East. It had been twelve moons since they'd last seen him.

Jack said Wind Flower was a fast learner and urged her parents to enroll her in the government school. "She'd outshine them all," Jack had told them, but Strong Arrow and Smooth Water wouldn't hear of it.

Hurrying to gather as many twigs and branches as she could, Wind Flower rushed back, frantic with worry and longing to comfort her sister.

Where were they taking them? There had been so many stories circulating among her people, tales of children abducted and sold into slavery in Mexico, but these men were not Mexicans. Who were they? Her kindred always spoke of the white man and his devilish ways in hushed tones, breaking off the talk when children appeared. She felt so ignorant, so unprepared.

Dropping the twigs in front of the man called Les, she moved toward her sister. "Not yet," he snarled pulling her back. "Fire first, then the kid." He used the Cheyenne word for fire, then repeated it. "Fire."

Wind Flower was experienced in fire starting, a chore that had been hers alone for many moons, and she soon had a small crackling fire blazing. The men brought food and cooking utensils from their saddlebags.

As they prepared dinner, she began inching her way toward Laughing Dove until she sat at her sister's side. She slid her arm around the trembling child, and Laughing Dove collapsed against her, sobbing. As the men appeared to take no notice of them, Wind Flower quietly slipped off the gag, and the muffled sobs became more audible.

Their captors turned, and Cooky yelled, "Hey," but the other man said, "If she can shut up, it can stay off. If not, back on it goes. Understand?" He gestured with his hands and Wind Flower nodded, whispering to her sister, beseeching her to be silent. After several great sighs and heavings of breath, her weeping ceased, and she lay shivering in her sister's arms.

As he pulled a tin pot from the stove, Cooky motioned to them. "Come, eat." They were each given a bowl of something called hash that burned their throats and tasted horrible. The girls tried to eat for fear of angering their captors, but the hash simply would not go down.

Finally, the men allowed them to retreat back from the fire to where their root bags lay forgotten on the ground. Wind Flower reached into hers for a turnip, intending to share it with Laughing Dove, but the cocking of a pistol stopped her.

"Not so fast." Cooky's gun was aimed at her heart, his eyes, cold and empty, glaring down at her. Killer's eyes.

"Put it down, Cooky." Les pushed his partner's hand away, then advanced toward the pair huddled on the ground. In their tongue, he asked, "What's in the bag?"

In reply, Wind Flower spilled the contents onto her skirt. When he spied the small stash of roots and berries, Les laughed. "Yep, Cooky, ya better shoot 'em! That there's a dangerous bunch of loot they got theirselves." Cookie scowled, turning back toward the fire, ignoring Les, who laughed until tears ran down his cheeks.

The girls chewed small pieces of turnip, comforted by the familiar taste after the putrid hash. They huddled together on a blanket the men had thrown them, until Les said, "Time to sleep, little ones. Don't you be scared, now. We's taking you to school. Understand? School? Not gonna scalp you or kill you. So you can rest easy."

In spite of her fears, sleep soon overtook Wind Flower, lulled as she was by the even, steady breathing of her sister beside her. Laughing Dove had fallen asleep with the turnip still in her mouth. Fallen asleep, midchew.

The man's words made no sense to Wind Flower. What did he mean about school? Was he taking them back to the reservation school? If so, why had they grabbed them in the first place?

ABOUT THE AUTHOR

M. Lee Prescott is the author of dozens of works of fiction for adults, young adults, and children, among them *Prepped to Kill*, *Gadfly*, *Lost in Spindle City*, and *Poof!* (Ricky Steele Mysteries), *A Friend of Silence*, *In the Name of Silence*, and *The Silence of Memory* (Roger and Bess Mysteries), *Jigsaw*, and *Song of the Spirit*, and her newest contemporary romance series, *Morgan's Run*, of which *Kyle's Journey* is the eighth! Three of her nonfiction titles have been published by Heinemann, and she has published numerous articles in the field of literacy education. Lee is a professor of education at a small New England liberal arts college, where she teaches reading and writing pedagogy. Her current research focuses on mindfulness and connections to reading and writing. She regularly teaches abroad, most recently in Singapore.

Lee has lived in southern California (loved those Laguna nights!), Chapel Hill, North Carolina, and various spots in Massachusetts and Rhode Island. Currently, she resides in Massachusetts on a beautiful river, where she canoes, swims, and watches an incredible variety of wildlife pass by. She is the mother of two grown sons and spends lots of time with them, their beautiful wives, and her beloved grandchildren. When not teaching or writing, Lee's passions revolve around family, yoga (Kripalu is a second home), swimming, sharing mindfulness with children and adults, and walking.

Lee loves to hear from readers. Email her at mleeprescott@gmail.com, and visit her website to hear the latest and sign up for her newsletters!

AUTHOR WEBPAGE AND NEWSLETTER SIGN-UP

http://www.mleeprescott.com

FOLLOW ME ON BOOKBUB!

https://www.bookbub.com/authors/m-lee-prescott

A NOTE FROM THE AUTHOR

I am so happy to bring you Kyle and Harriet love story! This marks the eighth of the *Morgan's Run* books and also a preview of my next series, the *Darn Yarners* which will debut in 2019! A contemporary romance series, the **Darn Yarners** follows Helen, Harriet and a host of strong, resilient women across the country to the New England coastal town of Horseshoe Crab Cove! Stay tuned for updates about the *Darn Yarners* and, of course, more **Morgan's Run** books too! Thank you so much for reading *Kyle's Journey* and returning with me to Saguaro Valley. As you know, the *Morgan's Run* books are set in the gorgeous American Southwest, an area of the country that is dear to my heart not only because it is home to my youngest son and family, but also because its beauty is so extraordinary and so startlingly different from that of my New England home. Now, I am so pleased to explore the beauty of the craggy New England coast with a village of colorful, vibrant characters as the *Darn Yarners* series begins!

If you like *Kyle's Journey* and would be willing to write an Amazon review, I would be very grateful. If you would like to sign up for future book releases, giveaways and occasional notices about my books, please visit my Author Website and sign up for my newsletter and follow me on BookBub. I promise I will not share your address, nor will I flood you with emails. Do visit my site to read more about my books and hear what's next.

Finally, this book has been revised, proofed, and edited many, many times, but my intrepid assistants and I are human, so if you spot a typo, please email me at mleeprescott@gmail.com, and I will fix it. If you'd like to know more about my other books, please scroll ahead to the next section.

Warm wishes,
M. Lee

OTHER BOOKS BY M. LEE PRESCOTT

Contemporary romances and mysteries by M. Lee Prescott include:

The Ricky Steele Mysteries
Book 1: *Prepped to Kill*
Book 2: *Gadfly*
Book 3: *Lost in Spindle City*
Book 4: *Poof!*

Also, featuring Ricky Steele:
Jigsaw

Roger and Bess Mysteries
Book 1: *A Friend of Silence*
Book 2: *In the Name of Silence*
Book 3: *The Silence of Memory*
Book 4: *Silencing the Pen* (coming in 2019!)

Contemporary Romances

Well-Loved Romances

Widow's Island

Hestor's Way

Morgan's Run Romances

Book 1: *Emma's Dream*

Book 2: *Lang's Return*

Book 3: *Jeb's Promise*

Book 4: *Rose's Choice*

Book 5: *Hope's Wonder*

Book 6: *Ruthie's Love*

Book 7: *Polly's Heart*

Book 8: *Kyle's Journey*

Young Adult Historical Romance

Song of the Spirit

www.ingramcontent.com/pod-product-compliance
Lightning Source LLC
Chambersburg PA
CBHW021005120726
47905CB00009B/2868